Copyright Matthew Cash
All rights reserved. No part
reproduced in any form or
inclusion of brief quotations in a review, without
permission in writing from the publisher. Each author
retains copyright of their own individual story.
This book is a work of fiction. The characters and situations
in this book are imaginary. No resemblance is intended
between these characters and any persons, living or dead.
This book is sold subject to the condition that it shall not,
by way of trade or otherwise, be lent, resold, hired out or
otherwise circulated without the publisher's prior consent
in any form or binding or cover other than that in which it
is published and without similar condition including this
condition being imposed on the subsequent purchaser
Published in Great Britain in 2022 by Matthew Cash
Burdizzo Books Walsall, UK

MATTHEW CASH

FRANKIE SAYS DIE

MATTHEW CASH

BURDIZZO BOOKS 2022

MATTHEW CASH

FRANKIE SAYS DIE

Foreword

First things first. THIS IS A HORROR BOOK. I loathe anything, and I really do mean *anything*, that gives...well...*anything* away about a book. There are so many books I've seen with subtle spoilers actually embedded into the fucking covers whether it's part of the synopsis, a quote, or, once, a built-in sticker {like a fake sticker but part of the cover} that ruin a book for me before I've even started it. If a book has 'surprise twists and turns' I don't want to know about them otherwise I'll be keeping my eyes open for them. If it has a shock ending, unless someone has ripped the last twenty-odd pages out of it I'll be expecting it now you've given the bloody game away. It's the same with trigger warnings; they are spoilers.
The only thing I want to know about a book, aside from title and author, is a very basic plot line. I don't want to know that Gabby gets buggered by a shire horse in the seventeenth chapter and that Julian the marmot accidentally mistakes a microwave for a time machine. I want to be shocked, horrified and disgusted by these things, I don't want any warning.
It would be like trying to sell a slasher book where you tell everybody the body count, how you should expect each person to die, and whether the antagonist carks it or not at the end.

A lot, and I mean a lot, of people seem to have issues with animals getting hurt in books. Babies can get catapulted into the fucking sun after being raped three ways by a pylon but don't you go hurting them fictional doggos! I love animals, I love people {until they prove themselves unlovable} but if a story I'm writing suddenly jumps up and says, "hey, Matty-Bob, you know what's needed right here, right now, slap bang in the middle of this motherfucking paragraph, don't you? Someone forcing a cobra up a goat's arsehole, that's what!" and I agree, then I'll write it in.

It's important to get all those triggers...umm...truggered, 1) it helps them become less triggery and makes YOU a stronger person, 2) what the fuck is the point in reading something that's going to leave you as flat as a zombie's heart rate, 3) unless you're reading something that's specifically TRUE it's not real no matter how much you fully immerse yourself into a story and its plot, and even if it were true you're reading about something that has happened, still sad and horrible maybe, but there's nothing you can do about it other than show it respect, learn from it and make sure it doesn't happen again, 4) due to bad upbringing some dogs can be dangerous cunts and a 'BAD DOG' might not always suffice to stop the little blighter from crunching that newborn baby's head up like an egg shell full of passata, and last but most definitely not least, 5) everyone knows that All Dogs Go To Heaven...Yes, even Cujo, *especially* Cujo.
Lassie didn't though, Lassie was a pretentious cunt.

There's a dog in this book, he may or may not get hurt whether he's a nice dog or a bit of a twat dog, I don't know as I've not actually started writing it yet, but rest assured

FRANKIE SAYS DIE

he's a-coming, looks like quite a happy little fellow too, but he could also be very good at acting.
Matty-Bob
September 2022

MATTHEW CASH

FRANKIE SAYS DIE

Prologue

1.

Five hundred years ago.

Francis Foster, Last of the Liver Eaters closes the skin-bound book. His whole legacy is a sham, the book completely worthless, a lie. He has done everything the rituals asked for, even found five men who were sensitive to the secrets of the universe to help hone and grow his skills. He has sacrificed more than enough of his own life experimenting in all kinds of debauchery, but still he is weak.
What is the point in being able to swap bodies with another? It isn't the kind of immortality he seeks. Certainly he has already lived a lot longer than his descendants, this is his third vessel but he is still susceptible to illness and death. If something befell him, like it did his ancestors, before he can perform the ritual, such a complex thing in itself, then that would be that. It will be over. He needs better odds than that, wants better odds than that. He craves true immortality, a body impervious to pain and damage. Power.

Six is a magic number. In the small hamlet of Brantham six men have proven this. Together their powers over the elements have made the land fruitful, and the people strong with their knowledge of natural medicines. They have kept their special part of the countryside protected from invasion and blight for over fifty years. All was well in the circle until one member wanted more.

Francis Foster has had enough of petty dalliances with paupers and their trivial warts and verrucas. Their ailments and problems bored him long ago. The magic his syndicate performs has grown tedious. Who cares about fertility and health? Francis Foster has bigger ideals, he wants life eternal. He knows there is other magic in the village, like the forbidden pit that draws people in after just one glimpse.

Magic is a neutral power, one of the oldest elements around, older than earth, wind, water and air and if you found yourself open enough to tap into it you could use it for good or for bad. Francis Foster has had enough of doing good. In a crazed psychotic rage he tears his family grimoire apart and burns it in the cellars of the richest house in the village, swearing and shrieking for the very fabric of reality to cough something up to answer his prayers.

In the bowels of Brantham Hall the other members of Foster's sect feel the tension in the air as something magical is happening that has nothing to do with them.

Horace Keeble bursts into the cellar, the others close behind him. All five spot Foster amidst the overturned barrels and straw-covered crates.

"What the bloody hell have you done this time, Frank?" sneers Philip Rapier, Lord of the hall they stand beneath. Francis Foster glints at them with sheer malevolence, his grey beard and hair is unkempt and drenched in sweat. He

FRANKIE SAYS DIE

points towards a far corner where a faint red glow tints the darkness.

"You best not have been meddling in anything untoward," Harold Meadows fingers the crucifix around his neck.

"You're all hypocrites," Foster snarls. "You all have so much already, you take, take, take." He looks at Keeble, "land." Rapier, "wealth." He grimaces at Meadows, the village preacher. "Faith and devotion."

"Even you have your looks and your way with the ladies," Foster hisses at Peter Willis, a fit, young farmhand, of Keeble's.

"And you with your game and falconry." He spits at Steven Colbear. "You're all rich without this added ability we've been gifted with. All of you, rich, apart from me." Foster clutches at his filthy rags. "It's time we thought of ourselves. Time we gathered the spoils for our good deeds."

"That's not how we work, Frank," Meadows whispers softly.

Francis Foster swipes his hands in front of his chest and the five men fall back, slammed by an unseen force. "It's how I work!"

"Enough!" Keeble shouts and pushes against the magical restraints.

Foster sighs and the men are freed.

"Let's see what you have done and whether we can put it right." Keeble moves past the cowering pauper and heads towards the red light. Cautiously the others follow.

In the darkness lying in a foetal position is a pale, naked man. His doughy flesh is blubbery, hairless and dimpled,

fat clings to him like a chubby baby. The red light comes from below his skin like a subcutaneous layer.
"It's just a man," Willis states, "a bloody fat one and all."
"If that's the best you can do on your own we've nothing to worry about," Steven Colbear jests and Willis joins him in laughter.
Foster grins as the hulk on the floor begins to move and the hellish glow dissipates.
"That's no man," Meadows says tearing the crucifix from his neck and starting to chant Latin.
It looks like a man though.
The figure stands on thick, stumpy legs and faces away from them. A long, seemingly endless gust is expelled from between its gigantic buttocks, it engulfs them in sulphuric poison. The men stumble and cough but Meadows holds firm, continuing the words of his exorcism.
The fat man's red light dims completely and he is only lit by the glow of the candles Foster has scattered.
They watch as he turns.
Like any other gluttonous male, a huge belly blooms over below-average-sized genitals. He is completely bald, has a serene, childlike face. He's like a dewinged grown-up cherub, but when he grins it is too wide, and his teeth too big, too white.
"Demon!" Meadows shouts and thrusts his cross like a weapon towards the man.
The man wheezes, his shoulders jostle up and down, his torso shakes and he lets out the belly-rippling laugh of an imbecile. A trickle of fluid dribbles from his shrivelled penis and onto his thigh.
Rapier looks at Foster disgustedly. "Get that thing out of my house."

FRANKIE SAYS DIE

Even Francis Foster appears disappointed at what he has brought forth from dimensions unknown.
"Is this what you were expecting?" Keeble asks, gesturing to the man with the idiot grin.
"What manner of being are you?" Foster can't contain his anger, his embarrassment, and despite this feat of trickery his fellow coven members begin to laugh at the result of his conjuring.

When the thing speaks its mouth stays fixed in the idiot grin, its jolly composure never moves. Its voice comes from somewhere else outside the room, maybe even this reality.
"I AM."
"What, what are you? Demon? Angel."
The thing continues to beam with foolish serenity. "There is no such thing. We from the Other are shaped by our conjurers."
"You've basically conjured a blank slate," Rapier snorts. "He looks strong though. Maybe he can pull your plough, Keeble."
Foster backs away, their laughter hits him like stones. What is the point of this thing if it can't give me knowledge greater than that I already know? I've conjured a useless hunk of flesh. Or have I? He thinks about what the thing said about the conjurer shaping the creature and petty vengeance fills his mind. He points at the other men. "If you can't teach me anything then please, feel free to roam the earth as you wish, take these fools with you though, make them your slaves. You're a demon, act like one."
The thing nods but still acts like a dribbling imbecile. Then something happens as the men lose themselves to their

mirth. The thing from another dimension is animated by the sound of their laughter, his eyes dart around the low-ceilinged cellar, his fingers snap in the air like he's trying to catch their laughs like butterflies. He's enthralled by the sound of their amusement, no, their actual feelings of hilarity. He feeds off it. He begins to change, his eyes sink further into his baby face and his smile becomes wider, wide enough to eat them all if he so desires. His nose swells like a rapid ripening fruit, mimicking their physical signs of merriment, capillaries explode across the surface making it gigantic and red. He waves a hand towards the frantic clergyman and Meadows screams as his crucifix changes into a severed penis.

"Yes!" Francis Foster cries. "Yes. Take them. Punish them for laughing at me, at you. Make them do what demons should do. Go out, maim and murder."

The thing nods and somehow his grin spreads even more.

Francis Foster's experiments have proven fruitful after all. This being is from somewhere new to them, birthed from a dimension that is nonsensical. His five cohorts are suspended, upside down in the air. The man from another dimension's mouth opens wider and wider and wider and there's no teeth there now just a never-ending spiral, a wormhole, a portal to another dimension. Deep within that forevermouth five stars appear and burn with red intensity. The five glowing orbs float from the depths of his maw and each penetrates an upturned man.

Once everything is quiet, once Francis Foster's friends have had their modifications, the fat man steps towards him and slaps his big hands against his colossal, jiggling belly.

FRANKIE SAYS DIE

Foster watches transfixed as the flesh across the lower half of the bulk splits open into a wide, wet, gory smile. Francis sits with him a while and teaches him all about malevolence and the correct manner in which demons should act.

MATTHEW CASH

FRANKIE SAYS DIE

2.

1976

Frankie grabs the lad with the pink Mohican by the upper arm, pulls him away from the pub and pushes him into the back of the blue and white Cortina.
"Fucking pig!" The punk spits as Frankie accidentally slams the door on his leg.
"Shut it. You're nicked already, don't make it worse for yourself."
"I didn't do anything," the kid says from the back of the car. His name is Arthur Dean, he's eighteen, Frankie knows everything about him.
"You were about to glass that Spurs fan who was taking the piss out of your hair," Frankie says, snatching a glimpse in the rear-view.
"You can't arrest me for something I was about to do," Arthur protests, "and besides, I wasn't."
Frankie cackles, "You had the broken handle in your hand ready." He sees Arthur's face pale.
"I was taking it to the bar. I dropped me glass, didn't I?"
"Bollocks," Frankie switches the radio on and turns the volume up.
He takes the back streets, knows the area well, it is on his beat, as is The First Round, the rough dive which they seem to pass off as a pub around this area.
It was after a night sat outside The Round that he first clocked Arthur and knew he would be the next in line.
"Where are you taking me?" Arthur moans from the back.

MATTHEW CASH

"The station in Ghimby, the one here's got too many idiots in there tonight." Frankie's impressed with the kid's sense of direction.

"Bloody hell, that's six miles away."

"If you're a good boy I'll give you the bus fare to get back in the morning."

"I don't want to spend the night in a cell. I've done nothing wrong."

Frankie turns in the seat. "I'm saving you from yourself, son. I know that look I saw in your eye outside The Round. If I'd come a minute later this would be a lot more serious, I'll bet."

The kid fell silent. Soon he began to doze. Frankie can see the amount of alcohol he has drunk has knocked him out. He'd be asleep any minute. That's the last thing he wants. Taking note that where they are is pretty secluded, he knows he is going to have to perform the ritual sooner rather than later. He slows the car and pulls up beside a darkened factory.

"What you doing?" Arthur's perked up and pushing himself towards the front of the car.

"Did you not hear that?" Frankie says annoyed, "fucking well run over something."

"You hit someone?" Arthur's wide awake now.

"Don't be daft. Probably a fox or something but it don't look good having a cop car covered in blood now does it? I'm just going to get out and make sure there's no mess." Frankie stifles a laugh as he climbs from the car, *make sure there's no mess, that's a good one*. He walks around to the trunk, opens it and takes the knife out.

"*Cashtella mogga…*" The moment the first few syllables of the chant leave his lips he feels the tingle. No one would notice it unless they were specifically in tune with these

FRANKIE SAYS DIE

things. Arthur looks confused as he sees Frankie open the rear door and is petrified when he sees the knife. "What are you doing?"
"Relax," Frankie reassures between the archaic mantra he sings, "I'm not going to hurt you, I promise."
An even fearful expression takes over the boy's face. "You're going to rape me, aren't you?"
Frankie laughs and kneels next to his captive. "I ain't one of them, son. No, I'm not going to touch you unless you don't do as you're told."
Frankie takes off his constable jacket, pulls his tie off and rips open his white shirt to reveal sweat-drenched, pale-white blubber. He really didn't pick wisely with the copper's body at all.
"What's that stuff you're saying? Are you mental?"
"*Klum neeha poltava poltove poltivia…*" The words come almost automatically, he knows the mantra by heart.
Without hesitation Frankie thrusts the knife into his own stomach, just below the ribs and pulls it down.
Arthur's scream rocks the car.

Frankie breathes, there's no pain but it's always the hardest part. His lips move at an alarming pace as he cuts and tears through the layers of fat on the copper's stomach.
Arthur is covered in blood and yellow clumps of fat, too frozen by the self-butchery to do, or say, anything.
"Don't you pass out on me," Frankie seethes and slaps the kid around the face. He slips his hand inside himself and pushes and prods until he feels what he's looking for.
It takes years of practice to be able to find your own liver by touch. Years of victims too.

MATTHEW CASH

Frankie ignores the unusual sensations of his guts slurping around as he grabs the organ and severs it with the knife. There's not much time left. Frankie increases the mantra, repeating the words as quickly as he can but making sure the pronunciations are on point.

He slices slithers off the liver in his hand and pushes the meat into Arthur's mouth. Arthur reacts, gags, fights against the handcuffs but Frankie clamps both hands over his mouth and he has no choice but to swallow.

The pain is beginning, a sign the magic is working, and Frankie has to hold on, has to carry on with the ritual until he knows it's taken hold. He crams more liver into Arthur's mouth and finally flops back as he feels it begin.

Now he knows the ritual is a success he gives up his hold over the body of the copper, lets it bleed out onto the upholstery.

Frankie sighs, words still flow from the copper's blood-speckled lips, and sees the sudden look of confusion as Arthur feels his alien presence invading him.

Frankie spits the remnants of the copper's liver from his mouth and kicks out at the disembowelled policeman. The fat ginger copper tumbles backwards from the Cortina and onto the road.

"Jesus," he says, trying out Arthur's voice for the first time, "glad to be out of that fat, old, bastard."

FRANKIE SAYS DIE

3.

2002

The last night of Greenfields Circus is always such a joyous time for the true magicians of the show. They have spent their time leaving thousands of people in child-like awe, rekindling magic they had long thought forgotten. Greenfields Circus is one of the last real magic circuses but real magic doesn't come cheap.
The magicians must show their real faces at least once at the end of each season. Those were the rules and these were the prices.
Ten year old Tommy knows some of what goes on at the circus, has seen the acts' real faces but doesn't understand the importance of the last night performance, doesn't understand who or what the Old Acts really are, but ringmaster Ray Greenfield keeps a close watch on the Boy Who Sees. "It's best you stay in your tent tonight, Tommy," Ray offers the boy reassurance. "And no matter what you hear, stay there until morning. Remember the Old Acts require special sustenance and payments for their wonderful performances."

"There you go, Boinky," comes the squawky voice of Mr Crackers, the stuffed parrot. "Glad Harry has fucked his legs up with his sledgehammer so he won't be able to run that fast now. Plus you and Jonathan got him a good one in the guts."

MATTHEW CASH

Boinky the clown grins. His grin is already exceptional without the tattooed green clown smile that outlines his mouth and spreads over his cheeks and ears like a leprous disease. Boinky prides himself on his dental hygiene, his teeth are perfect, even and white. Aside from the tattooed grin the rest of his face is covered in thick, messily-applied white makeup, his eyelids have eyes painted on them so it looks like he's always watching.

Even though the kid is built like a rugby player he is no match for Glad Harry and his hammer. But once the lad cops eyes on Boinky he somehow stumbles across the wet grass on his mashed-up feet. The sight of an excessively fat, almost-naked clown has made the boy shit himself.
Boinky stands stupidly transfixed at the waddling youth before pushing his chin down into his meaty chest and consulting a huge clown face which is tattooed over his torso.
Captain Flimbo, Boinky's name for the huge clown face that has his tits for eyes and his belly for its evil cackling mouth, wobbles excitedly and shouts encouragement. "Get 'im Boinkers, get 'im an' improvise," Captain Flimbo cackles like a depraved old man.
Boinky laughs merrily, stomping his feet in excitement, tightens his grip on Jonathan, his butcher's knife, and skips after the fleeing jock.
The lad has run into the helter-skelter, probably to hide. Boinky loves the helter-skelter. He hurries up the wooden stairs and sees the kid turn and laugh before facing the whirly, swirly slide.
Boinky's quick when he wants to be and he thrusts his hand forward and yanks a slippery coil of the kid's intestine out of the slash Jonathan made in his stomach and

FRANKIE SAYS DIE

Mr Crackers squawks with approval. The kid squeaks, Boinky laughs like an emphysemic Goofy and pushes him. The kid shrieks as he slides backwards down the helter-skelter, his innards unravelling with the downward trajectory.
"Great stuff, Boinko m'lad," says Mr Crackers, giving his pirate hat a wobble. Boinky laughs like Goofy again and wipes his hands on his pink tutu.
Boinky loves his pink tutu, the others at the circus tell him he should wear something else, they were fed up with seeing his cock and balls swinging about.
Boinky is proud of his cock and balls, it took him ages to tattoo them. Two happy round clown faces decorate his scrotum and his penis is swirled with red and green lines to match the stripes of Greenfields' Circus tent. The swollen tip has a flower tattooed around the opening like a squirting joke flower.
Mr Crackers found it difficult to settle on his shoulder when he and Boinky first became acquainted but the staples and stitches helped and Boinky couldn't even feel the pain anymore now the gangrene had set in.

"And now, the man you've all been waiting for—" booms a pre-recorded voice out of gigantic speakers that deafen the audience and drown out their screams. The recording stops and a man walks onto the stage and ends the announcement, "—the magical Mr Rapey."
Philip Rapier barely remembers his earthly existence now, recognises the face in the mirror but most of his essence is gone elsewhere, just enough left behind to witness the

obscenity which the being that inhabits him calls sustenance.

A chorus of shrieks and blood-curdling wails come from the dozen drunken rugby supporters roped to the chairs.
"Ey, that's no way to make a showman welcome now is it?" Mr Rapey removes his black top hat and sweeps it before him with an elaborate bow. With a white-gloved fingertip he pushes a button on a remote control and a pre-recorded audience whoops and cheers.
"That's better ain't it?" he says grinning through a mouth full of blackened teeth. He scratches his thick bushy black beard and looks at one of the real audience members.
"What's that John?" he winks at the others, "'What have I got in my hat?'"
A man thrashes in his chair, incapable of anything other than screaming.
Mr Rapey smiles, "Why, what does a magician usually find in his hat? Why a rabbit of course." He dips his hand into the hat and pulls out a big pink dildo complete with a clitoral stimulator. He pushes a button and the fake audience roars with laughter. Mr Rapey giggles and wiggles the dildo towards some of the ladies in the chairs.
"Ey, we'll have to see about making this vanish again later on, eh?" He waggles it against the crotch of his suit trousers and the fake crowd cackles and hollers.
"Now then, now then, calm down a little. You're a rowdy lot ain't you?" Mr Rapey smiles warmly and claps his hands together. Behind him a grubby curtain is drawn back to reveal a wheeled gurney; several luminescent stars have been glued to it in a half-arsed attempt at making it look magical. Bending over the table and securely bound is a naked woman.

FRANKIE SAYS DIE

"Now, I'd like you all to give a great big round of applause to Brenda here who I volunteered for this exceptional magic trick."

The screaming in the tent reaches a new crescendo, Mr Rapey ups the volume on the recording before pressing the button and once more drowning them out with the fake audience. Strange mystical music blares from the speakers as Mr Rapey waves his hands around, lifting the filthy cuffs of his sleeves to show they are empty, and spinning the table around to show them it's a real woman.

"Now, ladies and gentlemen, I have a sad story to tell you. This time last month my pride and joy, my pet rabbit Spunky, died of old age."

The fake audience makes a vaguely sympathetic noise, there's a scattering of laughter. Mr Rapey is offended, "Who laughed? It was a lot sadder than that." The speakers ring out with a far more sympathetic groan. "That's better, you bunch of heartless cunts," Mr Rapey chuckles.

He delves inside his hat and pulls out a rotting rabbit carcass by its ears. "As you can see, Spunky is well and truly dead." He raises the dripping bunny to his mouth and shouts, "Hello, I have carrots." The dead rabbit does nothing apart from shower maggots and lose another clump of mottled green fur.

"My friends, I learnt a powerful spell from my friend Omagh Shinowi the witch doctor and I am going to show you the miracle of resurrection."

The fake crowd oohs and ahhs whilst the real one struggles to free themselves from restraints that have no give. The woman on the table shrieks and her bowels and bladder sluice onto the floor. Completely oblivious, or maybe ever the professional showman, Mr Rapey continues his infamous trick. A trick he must perform at the end of every season. After scooping up what he can of the rotting Spunky he situates himself behind the lady. "Now, witness the stages of resurrection. First we must take the remains of that in which we hope to live again and," Mr Rapey forgets his lines, "err, shove 'em up her cunt."

The noise the woman makes on the table was like nothing any of the audience have ever heard. Mr Rapey spreads the woman's vaginal lips with two fingers and proceeds to push sloppy bits of decomposed rabbit up inside her. By the time he has forced the entire rabbit inside the woman has passed out. He looks disappointed and sticks out his bottom lip, "Aww, you're gonna miss the fun bit."

The fake audience cheer and wolf-whistle as Mr Rapey drops his trousers and displays his proud erection. "How's that for a magic wand, Harry Potter?"

The fakes laugh, Mr Rapey laughs, his cock jiggles up and down.

"Now," he exclaims, serious and dramatic, "the gift of life." Mr Rapey thrusts himself into the woman's gaping, ruined, gore-stuffed hole.

"Ey, Spunky, move over a little, will you?" More canned laughter as Mr Rapey gets comfortable and begins a steady fucking rhythm. Mr Rapey bares his teeth and digs his fingers into the woman's buttocks and ejaculates inside her. "The gift," he pants, "of life." He swipes sweat from his brow on his sleeve and catches his breath. When he pulls out his gore-covered penis a disgusting red blancmange of offal and sperm glop onto the floor. Not bothering to clean himself, he yanks up his trousers and addresses the audience. "And now for the resurrection bit."

FRANKIE SAYS DIE

An almost silent scream comes from his passed-out volunteer as she regains consciousness just in time for the finale. The woman's eyes widen and she retches up a lump of bloodied tissue. Her shoulders shake and her face darkens as she starts choking.
Several members of the real audience have passed out, some are violently throwing up onto the sawdust floor. Mr Rapey crouches and peers into the woman's open mouth. "That's it, love, you're doing grand."
The woman's throat bulges unnaturally and she luckily loses consciousness through lack of oxygen and internal bleeding as a long purple thing begins to push its way out of her mouth. It seems to be struggling with the small exit but after a loud crunch of breaking bone, the woman's jaw breaks and the thing slops onto the table. Mr Rapey quickly wipes slimy purple goo from the lump, a sticky amniotic caul. The fully-grown white rabbit twitches its nose at the audience. Mr Rapey kisses it on the head and holds it up to the audience and awaits their applause.

Locked deep within this everlasting carcass Lord Philip Rapier screams and curses the name of Francis Foster.

Dead centre in the middle of the circus stands the lighthouse, a tall wooden tower painted red and white wrapped around a rickety spiral staircase. At the summit of this erection is a large beacon and a fenced off platform. This is where Albatross Steve roosts. On the ground, several hundred feet below, the muddied grass is littered with adolescent bodies in various stages of devastation, and feathers which have been trampled into the sod. Albatross Steve stands on the platform, the chill night wind ruffling the feathers around his head. He adjusts the bright-yellow prosthetic beak that is attached to his mouth and nose with elastic, pulls it away and spits over the edge. Down below he sees Glad Harry and his crew frog-march the young fledgelings towards the entrance of the lighthouse. He sticks his beak back on, caws excitedly and flaps his wings. For a second he sees the falcons he raised from chicks as a man, watches pheasant and partridge making merry amongst the furrows.

Maybe this time one of my children will learn.

It takes the fledgelings nearly half an hour to climb the tower, he hears Glad Harry shouting at them to hurry up as they ascend. Albatross Steve drops his feathered grey jodhpurs and ejects a stream of liquid shit over the edge of the platform.

The first fledgeling is presented to him by one of Glad Harry's congregation, Gormless Pete, a big brute of a man with the mind and clothes of a baby and zero recollection of the attractive young farmhand he was in a previous existence.

"Birdie man," Gormless Pete says through a toothless grin and pushes the naked child towards him.

Albatross Steve regards the fledgeling before him.

As instructed, every inch of the child's naked body is covered white and grey downy feathers. His sobs are muffled behind the orange beak glued to his mouth. Snot bubbles leak and pop onto the crude mask.

FRANKIE SAYS DIE

Albatross Steve spreads his twelve-foot wingspan and nods towards the edge of the platform. "It is time to fly," he sounds well-spoken, like a thespian.
The kid hesitates and is awarded with a double-handed prod by Gormless Pete and pushed over the side.
"Fly, fly. Fly," Albatross Steve shouts as the feathered child falls, pinwheeling to the mud with a wet crunch.
"Nooo!" Albatross Steve sighs, broken behind his beak, and turns away from the edge. No bird likes to see their fledglings fail.
He nods to Gormless Pete, "Next."
One day, one day I'll have a fledgeling that flies.

Horace Keeble was the one who kept the most of his soul after the demon, or whatever it was, took over. Now he can only experience life through the thing that changes its face from performer to demon.

Farmer Spacklecock is a handsome man. Standing in green Wellington boots, corduroy trousers, green gilet, shirt, cravat and flat cap he looks like a rustic hipster.
His audience cowers in the tent against a wall of hay bales, their arms and legs bound tightly.
He whips a sheet off a ten-foot high wheel. On the wheel farmyard animals have been painted in the different marked out sections. A spade handle juts from the ground, a makeshift pointer. "Welcome to my farm game," the Farmer says and waves a hand over the wheel. "Will you be lucky enough to lay an egg with the chickens? Help shear the sheep of their woollen coats and skin? Milk the

bull? Feed the pigs? Go to a donkey party? Or perhaps have fun horse-riding?" He clutches the wheel in both hands. "We shall see."

The wheel clacks as it spins, the different farm animals whizz past the shovel handle pointer. Farmer Spacklecock peruses the crowd against the hay and gestures to one of Glad Harry's men to his chosen contestant. A chunky bald man is brought up before the wheel, his binds cut.

"Good evening sir," Farmer Spacklecock beams like a quiz show host. "And what's your name?"

"Please," the man, on his knees, pleads. "Please let me go."

"Well, Mr Letmego, are you feeling lucky tonight? Is there an animal you've got your money on?"

The man weeps. "You're all insane."

"The chickens?" Farmer Spacklecock smirks at the audience and nods to the spinning wheel. "Why is it never the chickens? It's the horse of course."

He grabs the wheel and adjusts it so it stops with the horse symbol resting behind the spade handle.

The man falls to the floor and is kicked in the ribs by the farmer. "Now, whilst Glad Harry's boys get you ready, I'll go set up the show jumping." Farmer Spacklecock nods to the men standing by and pushes the wheel to the back of the barn.

Glad Harry's men roll the man onto his back and whilst three of them hold him down one of them straddles his waist and begins. Glad Harry's goon takes a small horseshoe, presses it against the man's knee and takes a three-inch nail from his lips. The man is still screaming from the first nail when the goon starts on the second knee. They have just fitted the last horseshoe to the man's hands when Farmer Spacklecock returns.

FRANKIE SAYS DIE

"Ah, what a thoroughbred specimen we have here." He is dressed from head to toe in riding gear, complete with a red show-jumping jacket.

The man is forced onto his hands and knees even though they can barely support him. A pitiful wail comes from him and Farmer Spacklecock fastens a specially made bit, a long blade with a chain attached at each end, into the man's mouth.

"I hope you don't mind me riding bareback," Farmer Spacklecock says as he straddles the man's back. He pulls gently on the chain behind the man's head. The blade slices the corners of his mouth.

"Gee up horsey. Get through the jumps and you can have a nice long rest."

Instead of the usual hurdles the horses would jump over, swords are positioned on their sides a few inches off the ground.

"Gee up horsey," Farmer Spacklecock says sternly into the man's ear. The man crawls weakly towards the first fence and even though the pain he is suffering is excruciating somehow he makes it over the first hurdle.

"Well done, such grace and elegance," Farmer Spacklecock congratulates him and pats his shoulder.

The next hurdle is a bit higher and although the man feels the sword edge scrape a few layers of skin from his belly he succeeds in clearing the jump.

He slumps to the ground, Farmer Spacklecock yanks hard on the chain slicing his cheeks to the jaw.

It is the last hurdle that lets the man down. Weakened from pain, blood loss causes him to falter as he lifts his arms over the sword. He slips and the blade sinks into the

flesh above his wrist and slices upwards to his elbow. He bawls and screams and rolls to the floor knocking Farmer Spacklecock onto the sawdust.
Farmer Spacklecock brushes himself off and observes the man's ruined arm. "What use is a lame horse?"
The man lays on the crowd clutching his arm to his side weeping uncontrollably. "Chin up matey," Farmer Spacklecock says sympathetically and raises the man's chin with a fingertip. "Give us a smile." With that, he runs a knife across the man's throat and watches him die.
It is always sad when an animal doesn't make it.

FRANKIE SAYS DIE

4.

NOW

Georgina Vickers is glad that it's not the hot veterinary practitioner this time, the one that looks like someone took Jason Momoa, got rid of all those gross hard bulgey bits and swapped them with some more wibbly bulgey bits. The vet she's seeing today is the lady one, not that that really matters as far as Georgina Vickers' sexual preference goes. The lady vet is a fucking harpy if ever she saw one, she's about ten foot tall and her hair is scraped back so severely that her eyes are almost on the back of her head. Once, when Georgina was in infant school, she read an old kid's book called George's Marvellous Medicine by a really famous author. She loved the guy's books, liked how fucked up they were. This book was, to cut a short story shorter, all about a little boy who basically tried to poison his grandmother by throwing everything he could find in a saucepan and making a new medicine to swap with her old one. In it his grandmother grew all long and spindly, head sticking out of the chimney, arms out of the windows, that sort of thing, and there were fantastic pictures to accompany the tale. Well, the vet Georgina was due to see reminded her of those drawings, she was like a stork or heron and the most hilarious part of it all was her surname was Bird.
Georgina wasn't going to the vets to give the willowy Dr Bird some marvellous medicine but to hopefully get some off her.

MATTHEW CASH

Georgina's partner in crime sat on the chair beside her, his front legs resting on her thigh as he licked at a patch of fur just above his paw. He'd been licking the same place for at least five minutes and the waiting room was so quiet she could hear every squelch, gulp and grunt. With each lick she could feel the material of her jeans getting warmer and wetter. It was an endurance test just to see how long she could listen to the noise before the tingly feeling in her belly and chest shot up her spine, into her head and made her shout for him to stop. It was even worse when he was cleaning his dick.

"Zee," Georgina snaps, quietly so the receptionist doesn't hear. "Shuddafuckup!" But Zee, or Zoltan, was in the zone, she'd have to be more obvious than that. She rubs the muscle above his collar at the top of his spine and he stops licking immediately, his eyes half-closed and releases a moan of pleasure as she kneads him like dough.

"You're a good boy, aren't you?"

At the moment he doesn't give a shit what kind of boy he is as long as she keeps massaging his neck.

She smiles at him and feels a warm glow inside her that's tinged with more than a little sadness.

She was just starting high school when her parents got the two-toned brown dachshund for her as a puppy and he really was her best friend. They grew up together, he had helped her through plenty of shitty times at school and it was like they were part of each other. They knew each other's sounds and smells and emotions better than anyone else. Georgina hates bringing him to the vets, even when it's the hot one, as now he is almost a teenager in human years, she has his death on her mind.

What would she do without him? How would she cope? He was her shadow.

FRANKIE SAYS DIE

To make matters worse she sees his face every time she goes into Humphries' Everyday Essentials as they use him as their doggy model for the pet food section. His beautiful chocolate and beige face covers a whole fucking wall, he never has to pay for their brand of dog food either but typical of Zee he hates it with every fibre in his body. Georgina donates it to the kennels she works at.
But despite being an awkward, annoying, anti-sociable, finicky, lazy bastard of a dog she loves him to pieces.

MATTHEW CASH

FRANKIE SAYS DIE

Chapter One

The body in the mirror hasn't got long left, the doctors have confirmed that, plus it's getting old.
However, Frankie Foster's fond of this one, it has served him well since he took over residency from its previous owner forty-six years before.
"Good breeding," he says, taking in every line and wrinkle on the face. It looks twenty years younger than it's sixty-four years. That is Frankie's doing.
When he commandeered this vehicle it belonged to a leary punk on the other side of the country, but when Frankie got in the driving seat he got rid of all that shit, all the daft clothing and silly hair, so he could blend in better.

The great thing about soul transference is you have the next life already set up for you, identities, funds and everything. You have to choose well though. When buying a used car it is always advisable to give it a good once over inside and out before deciding to risk your money and your life in it. This one had been as fit as a fiddle; he could've been in the bloody army if it hadn't been for the anarchist wave washing the world at the time. But now the old motor was on its last legs, bodywork riddled with rust. It was time to trade it in.

When Frankie took the body of Arthur Dean for a routine check-up the doctor found an abnormality which led to further abnormalities and he was given the expectancy of six months tops. Frankie had always refused medication

and wouldn't start taking any now. There was no point, he wasn't worried.
He knows he has hung on to this one too long. He's grown comfortable in it, that's the problem, knows all its nooks and crannies, has enjoyed endless fun times in it, loves its nondescript features. You can't be a successful serial killer unless you've got good camouflage.

Frankie dresses Arthur's body in t-shirt, jeans and trainers and picks up his leather satchel. Inside the satchel is his and Arthur's life savings, the kid's parents died in the nineties and left him a packet. Frankie is a master of his craft, always tracks his next body for months, learning their routines, their mannerisms, their social circles. He was Arthur to the people Arthur had in his life until their stories came to natural endings. It's how he fooled the kid's family. They never suspected a thing, who would?

Frankie looks around his apartment one last time, mournful, but excited to shed this failing facade and slip into someone more comfortable.

It's been at least one hundred years since he was last a woman and something just told him that the time was right for a proper upheaval. After his brief, but glorious stint as the infamous serial killer, known as Jack the Ripper, he transferred to the body of one of Whitechapel's working girls, just so he could still float around observing the mayhem he had created. When he was Julie, it was the first time in his three hundred and twenty-seven years of slaughtering people for fun that he had taken a sabbatical. Five years off to collect his thoughts before a whirlwind of murders and swapping back into a man again.

FRANKIE SAYS DIE

Frankie sits in his car outside Man's Best Friend Kennels waiting for the day staff to knock off. He's not too inconspicuous, doesn't care about the consequences, and knows how the story will pan out. Same shit as last time.

Chapter Two

Georgina Vickers appears to be a young waif of a girl. She's small-framed with Nordic looks. She's elfin. Frankie doesn't know why he picked her; she just looks like someone he'd happily spend a few years inside.
She's twenty-two and wears gigantic headphones as she goes to and from work on the number ninety bus. He's seen all types over his years and heard all sorts of music and the stuff that blares out of those headphones when she gets on his bus to ride home every morning sounds bloody satanic, nothing at all like her exterior. She's always in her own world, hands thrust deep into the pockets of a green parka that almost buries her.

Frankie has done his research, he's been watching her for weeks, he takes so much more time and caution when planning his next swap, a lot more than when he's finding a potential victim.

There's a newspaper on the dashboard of his car, he's read the front page five times, allowing himself to feel sentimental at the end of yet another era. The headlines tell England that THE SMILER HAS STRUCK AGAIN. They don't know it was his last murder as The Smiler. It has been his longest spanning spree to date. Forty-five years. He made sure to leave plenty of evidence on the last one, just to confuse the fuck out of the fuzz when they finally find Arthur Dean's corpse.

Frankie takes his bag and leaves the car. The last of the day shift left Man's Best Friend an hour ago. The main building at the kennels is dark. He knows her routine, and heard a couple of the day shift taking the piss out of her on his bus. She spends the night talking to the dogs, playing music to them, petting them, making sure they aren't lonely and sad. Aw. That is probably one of the reasons he chose her, night work was good, easy, and he could plan what the next era would be. Maybe someone who targets young men, mutilates them, cuts off their dicks and stuff. Frankie doesn't care how he kills as long as he does it regularly. And Georgina looks like she could get away with anything. When he's her he can pop out when the pubs are closing, lure some drunken idiot with that hot, young body of hers, have some fun and be back for knocking off when the day shift comes in.

Frankie already set this plan in motion. The Smiler's last victim had a dog, a sappy fucking thing, and after he had left a permanent grin on the owner's face he took the dog for a holiday at the kennels. It doesn't matter that he is leaving a trail, this story is ending tonight.
Frankie presses the afterhours bell.

Chapter Three

"Hello?"
"Hello there," Frankie says into the intercom. "I'm Mr Dean. I'm sorry to call after hours but I've returned from my holiday earlier than expected so I'm here to pick my dog up."
"We can't reimburse you for the two days you have left."
"That's fine."
"Okay," Georgina mumbles, she sounds disappointed, like she wants to keep all the dogs for herself. "I'll let you in. Please wait in the waiting area and I'll bring Spartan to you."
"Thank you." Frankie waits for the door to unlock, thinks about what a stupid fucking name Spartan is for a chihuahua and makes a mental note to feed the bloody thing to a rottweiler once he is in charge of Georgina.
The buzzer wails, he enters the building and heads towards the waiting room. He takes a knife from his satchel, slides the bag beneath the seats and waits. The adrenaline begins to pump up inside him and he runs through the mantra in his head. Like he could ever forget it. Footsteps echo down the corridor but stop before they reach him.
"Sorry, I forgot the paperwork," Georgina calls.
There's music playing somewhere, heavy metal.
The bloody animals won't be listening to that when I'm in charge. He risks a peek around the corner of the waiting room, clocks the girl's arse in her yoga pants as she retreats

and knows she's going to pull loads of future victims. It's not until he hears her returning that he realises she never had the dog with her.

Something's up.

Why didn't she have the dog? A smile creeps to his lips, maybe the fictional rottweiler got the yappy little bastard after all. That would be hilarious.

Georgina returns and he holds the knife against the back of his leg. She still hasn't got the dog, just a stack of forms.

"Where's Spartan?" he asks faking concern.

Georgina can't meet his eyes and just holds onto the papers. "Oh, he's still asleep. I thought we could go down and get him once you've filled out the paperwork."

The last thing on Frankie's mind is paperwork, he opens his mouth to begin the chant when Georgina thrusts the sheets into his hands and jogs back down the hall.

"I'll just go wake him up and give him something to eat whilst you fill those in," she calls over her shoulder.

Frankie throws the paper to the floor. His intuition definitely tells him something is up. The girl is stalling. A vehicle stops outside. He prizes open the blinds and sees a police van. For a long second he's actually gobsmacked.

"The fucking bitch. How?"

A door slams at the end of the corridor and he storms towards it.

The door isn't locked, she's just done it to stall him, and knows the cops are here. He bursts through the reception area and sees her run towards the kennels. She's on the phone to someone.

The police are at the main door, trying to kick it in. Frankie quickens his pace and follows her into the kennels, it's one straight line with a dead end, there's nowhere for her to

FRANKIE SAYS DIE

run. She looks frightened as he storms towards her, knife in hand.

"The police are here!" she shouts, her hand rests on one of the kennel door handles.

He doesn't break his stride, can't afford to. He begins the mantra, "*Cashtella mogga blixa f'loggon…*"

Georgina opens the kennel and Frankie readies himself to have to fight off a potential dog attack but she vanishes inside the room.

All around, up and down the corridor, the dogs are going mental, teeth gnash and claws scratch.

Frankie braces himself for what breed of canine she's hiding with and enters the kennel.

Chapter Four

"For fuck's sake!" Frankie says and despite his predicament can't help but laugh. It's a fucking dachshund. The daft brown thing cowers behind Georgina, tail between its legs. He wastes no time, shouts his mantra, strides across the room, over the snow drift of cotton wool that the dog has ripped out of some stuffed toy, towards the frightened girl who surprisingly moves her foot up lightning quick and kicks him in the jaw.

He lands on his back on top of the dog food dishes and now the cowardly little bastard dog is barking and tugging at his trouser leg.

Georgina stands over him like a marvel hero grinning. "The dog's fucking microchipped, fucker," she says with triumphant glee. "The police have been tracking you since you brought him in."

"Bitch," Frankie wails and hears the police enter the building. Thoughts of having to pull the ritual in jail fleetingly cross his mind. There's still time. He says the words over and over as quickly as he can, and throws one of the ceramic dog food bowls at Georgina's head. It strikes her hard and she crumples to the floor dazed.

He's on her immediately. Straddling her with his knees he lifts up his t-shirt and cuts himself open.

The police are coming.

He finds his liver within seconds and cuts a chunk off. His lips are a blur as he says the mantra over and over again. He ignores the approaching police, ignores Georgina's disgusted screams as she beats at him with her fists, and ignores the pain. He grabs at her jaw, opens her mouth wide and forces the chunk of meat inside.

The cops burst into the room and pull him off of Georgina. One of them screams down their radio for a paramedic whilst they try to find something to stop the gash in his belly but it's okay, Frankie can feel the transfer beginning to work. He relaxes, allowing the death of this body to come quickly. He looks at Georgina, blood around her lips, spitting on the ground. It's not right, she should be the same as him, weak, getting ready for her soul to leave her body and make way for him. Frankie sees the dachshund lying on its side, breathing shallow, blood around its muzzle.

FRANKIE SAYS DIE

Chapter Five

Tommy gathers his blankets and rolls them into a bundle. He needs to leave the Job Centre doorway before the first workers arrive or they'll have a go at him. He's slept crap and his body is a stop motion puppet of knots and aches. The police are still at the kennels across the road, he doesn't know what went down there other than he must have been asleep when it started. He likes sleeping to the sound of dogs barking, they're his favourite animal, once he gets out of the hole he's in he's going to get one.
Tommy moves on to his spot on a walkway along the High Street at the back of the arcade, usually he can cadge a few coffees off the commuters and the blonde girl from the kennels sometimes stops and speaks to him as she goes to catch her bus. He wouldn't mind someone like that too, once he's back on his feet. Despite living on the streets for well over a decade he's forever optimistic that something will come up and change everything.
"Alright lad."
Tommy flinches at the sound of the voice, it's Norman, the oldest Hell's Angel in town, a local who always ventures out early morning to get his bits for the day. He's all wrinkles and flappy skin with a great big moustache like a walrus or tamarin monkey, and ancient motorcycle leathers. Tommy made the mistake of telling him his life story a few years ago and now he stops regularly.

MATTHEW CASH

"Hello, Norman," Tommy says, avoiding eye contact. Norman never gives him anything unless he gets something in return, but it's always good to be polite. "Do us a favour?"

Tommy hides his grimace as he sets his bedding down. He gets down and peers up at the old man. "What's up?"

Norman pulls his leather shopping trolley, decorated in heavy metal band patches, towards his tummy and flattens himself against the arcade window. Paper cut-outs of pound coins dangle behind him. He lets a few commuters pass before he speaks. "Want you to do me a reading, don't I?"

Tommy studies his dirty fingernails. He told Norman about his gift, amongst other things, and he's regretted it ever since. "This early in the day?"

"Come on," Norman pleads. "I'll shout you breakfast at the Wetherspoons."

The thought of a hot meal is tempting, it has been several days since he has eaten anything warm. Tommy sighs, "Okay, but it's still going to cost you twenty."

Norman smiles. "Mate, you are worth every penny. Come on."

Tommy pushes himself up off the floor. He looks forward to the meal and money but not the pain he is about to endure.

They leave the covered walkway and he sees the blonde lady from the kennels being loaded into a police car and feels a pang of sadness at seeing someone like her in trouble with the law.

It hurt, well it hurt him, reading people, telling them their fortunes. Norman waffles on and on about this new, to use

FRANKIE SAYS DIE

his phrase, *dollybird*, that he's started chatting to and wants to know what the future holds for him.
Tommy pities the old man, he just wants companionship, someone to watch telly with, share a scone and a cup of tea, nothing physical at his age other than a peck on the cheek and a cuddle. Norman only ever asks him to tell him about trivial things, nothing to do with illness, fortune or death but that doesn't stop Tommy from seeing it whenever he reads him. Tommy could charge for his service, make money from it like he did when he was a kid travelling with Greenfield's Circus, and he would too if it wasn't for the aftermath.

They find a quiet corner in the pub; breakfast is had and Tommy realises now his stomach is churning that he should have taken a rain check on the food. If he throws it up it would have been completely pointless, and they probably won't let him back in the pub either.

It's now or never, he prays he doesn't puke. Tommy lightly grips the handles of Norman's shopping trolley; all he needs to read is something someone has touched recently. Norman hasn't told him anything about this dollybird but Tommy sees she's on his mind straight away.
"Ey, Norman, she's a bit young for you, ain't she?" Tommy says with a sly grin. The lady looks at least ten years younger than Norman, her hair only starting to go white.
"I'm only sixty-nine. Age doesn't matter when it comes to true love, Tommy."
There's a gold necklace against her throat with Gloria on it. Tommy says the name aloud.

MATTHEW CASH

"That's her! You're the best, Tommy," Norman's getting excited now.

Tommy closes his eyes, tries not to let any emotion show as he gazes into wherever it is to see more of the scene. The scene has changed. The name is now on a floral wreath, Gloria is lying dead against white silk, the coffin is surrounded by lilies. Mourners stop at the casket to pay their respects, one of them is Norman, he's lost a lot of weight, he leans to plant a kiss on Gloria's cold cheek. Tommy notices a silver ring on Norman's wedding finger and smiles.

"What, what is it?" Norman begs.

Tommy pulls himself away from the future glimpses, the knives in his head already beginning to stab. "She's a keeper, Norman, spend as much time as you can with her. It's real."

"Finally," Norman whispers, tears in his eyes. He grips Tommy's hand tightly.

"Buy her lilies. She loves lilies," Tommy winces and presses his fingertips to his temples.

"Thank you, Tommy, thank you." Norman presses a twenty-pound note into his palm and goes to the bar to get them both a drink. For Tommy it'll be the first of many. He hangs his head in his hands and fights back the oncoming nausea.

Chapter Six

He looks like a hippopotamus cosplaying Donald Trump. Georgina has never been able to control her brain, it's like the damn thing has got a tiny little brain of its own. Same as her mouth. Quite often she's too scared to speak for fear of what might come out, she's usually the first to hear it and is normally just as shocked as the person she's talking to.

"How long have I got to sit in this shit hole? It smells like oniony farts and wank tissues." She wipes her palms over her face and smiles awkwardly, "Sorry, I'm just tired and in shock."

The hippo policeman, who did tell her his name but she was too busy studying the wiry hairs sprouting from his left nostril - one had a little green bogey clinging to it like a ball of nectar, smiled his hippo-smile and nudged the other cop.

The other cop was even worse. Even harder for Georgina to concentrate on. He was a dead-ringer for Tom Hardy. She was a horny twenty-two-year-old who hadn't had sex for at least fourteen hours and the last time was only with herself. She tried really hard to catch his name but when he spoke all she could think about was clinging onto his ears and riding his face like it was a bucking bronco.

"Miss Vickers," Hardy says, showing crooked teeth that she wanted nibbling her nether regions. "This is a simple procedure. We value your help in this case. We just need you to tell us, in your own words, what happened."

"My own words?" She asks unsure.
"That's right," Hardy and Hippo nod, giving their reassurance.
"Was he The Smiler?" Georgina had been following the case for the last few months since his apparent resurgence in this part of the country.
The Smiler had been a nightmarish enough name when she was a kid, an unknown serial killer who slit his victims' throats before slicing their cheeks into a Cheshire Cat grin.
"We can neither confirm or deny that as yet," Hippo states, he sounds like he gargles with mud.
"Well, he's definitely old enough. The Smiler's been around since the seventies."
"As my colleague says, Miss Vickers, we can neither confirm or deny that," Hardy smiles.
"It was so him." Georgina sits back feeling smug. She's caught a fucking serial killer.
"In your own words, Miss Vickers," Hardy reminds her.
"Right, well, when Mr Dean, aka The Smiler," she notes the looks of distain on the policemen and adds, "possibly, brought in Spartan—"
"I'm sorry, Spartan?" Hippo asks.
"Spartan the chihuahua, duh? Last Smiler victim's dog that went missing from the scene of the crime."
"Ah," Hippo says and laughs awkwardly, "I thought it was an apple."
Georgina frowns at him like he's a lunatic. "Why the fuck would a serial killer bring an apple to a kennels?"
"Er, he wouldn't."
"I mean he might, in case he got hungry, or he really was completely insane." Georgina momentarily lost her connection with reality as she pictured different serial

FRANKIE SAYS DIE

killers taking random fruit to a kennels for some insane reason only the nuttiest of serial killers would understand.
"Can we please stick to the matter in hand, Miss Vickers?" Hardy raises his voice, sounds all masterful and it really doesn't help matters.
"Sorry," Georgina tries to give him her nice smile, the one she hopes doesn't look too toothy and predatory. She clears her throat. "Mr Dean brought Spartan in last Thursday, as you know. That was when I informed you that he, Spartan, was the missing dog from the murder scene."
"And you found that out how?" Hardy asks.
"Whoever the victim was, was a good guy when it came to his pupper. Had him chipped and everything, all vaccines up to date.
"Well, when The Smiler—"
"Miss Vickers," Hardy says sternly and she melts, "can you not refer to Mr Dean as The Smiler for the sake of this statement please?"
"You said you wanted this in my own words."
Hardy sighs, "That's right. I apologise, carry on, please."
She thought she made the whip sound effect and gesture in her head but the fact that Hippo is laughing and Hardy is blushing a little suggests otherwise. She lets her mouth carry on whilst she prays for the ground to swallow her up. "The Smiler came in last night around seven, two days early, to pick Spartan up. I did as I was informed and phoned the number you guys gave me immediately and spoke to someone—"
"That was me," Hardy informs her.
"Oh, right, ummm," she pauses, not knowing what to do with this information. "Well done.

MATTHEW CASH

"Anyway, I knew you guys would like, rush over here straight away so I decided to try and stall him with some heavy paper work but he must have sussed shit was going down as he came after me. I saw him coming after me and that he'd got this great big, fuck-off knife. I went into the kennels with the intention of hiding until you pi- licemen, lol, nearly said pigs then," the laugh that comes out even sounds like a pig's snort which sets her off.

"When you're ready, Miss Vickers." Hippo loosens his collar.

"Soz," she points to her mouth, "this thing has a mind of its own." She winks at Hardy and wishes she was dead. "I was playing it by ear really, I didn't know what to do, so I hid in the nearest kennel. Stupid really as none of the doors lock from the inside."

"Then what happened?" Hardy asks frantically writing down what she's said so far.

"He bursts into the room and he's muttering all this mumbo-jumbo bollocks."

"Another language?" Hippo suggests.

Georgina shrugs, "I don't think so. If it was, I didn't recognise it, I could barely hear him other than he repeated the same shite over and over again as he came towards me. Zoltan was hiding behind me."

"I'm sorry? Who the fu— on earth is Zoltan?" Hardy snaps but corrects himself.

"Oh, he's my dachshund. He comes to work with me and stays in one of the rooms. That's whose kennel I was hiding in."

"I thought it was a Chihuahua?"

"No," Hippo rolls his eyes, "that's Spartan." Georgina grins, "See? My boy Hip—here knows the score. Keep up." Hippo blushes.

FRANKIE SAYS DIE

"Well, then, I remembered I do kickboxing and stopped acting like a fucking pussy and kicked him in the motherfucking face like a badass motherfucker!"
"Is profanity necessary?" Hardy shakes his head.
"My own words, bro. My. Own. Words."
"Carry on."
"Well, The Smiler lands on his arse in Zoltan's food bowl and that's about the only thing Zoltan will get arsey about so he's there tugging at The Smiler's trouser cuffs like fucking Cujo."
Hardy sighs. "Who's Cujo?"
"Saint Bernard. Has rabies. Stephen King," Georgina shoots facts like bullets.
"Wait, there was a Saint Bernard and someone called Stephen King there too? Is Mr King another member of staff? Where did he go?"
Georgina shuts her eyes and eradicates all sexual imagery of Hardy from her mind. "It was an expression. Cujo was a dog from a Stephen King horror book—"
"And film," Hippo adds.
"Dude," Georgina smirks and holds her hand up for a high five. She can see Hippo considers it but Hardy's looking at them like a couple of idiots.
"I'll make it simpler," she purrs and scowls at Hardy, "for you. The Smiler is on the floor, okay? And whilst he's down there he picks up one of Zoltan's food bowls and Frisbees the cunt, sorry, thing, at my head, where I got this." She points at the gauze on her forehead, "then he straddles me and I'm thinking 'ew, don't you fucking dare rape me,' but he lifts his shirt and slices his own guts open. All the time he's muttering voodoo shit. Then, get this, he

reaches into himself, hacks a bit of his lung off or some shit and forces it into my mouth."
The two policemen pale.
"That's when the cavalry arrive and pull him off me. I spat the crap out of my mouth and Zoltan ate it."
"Is that it?" Hardy asks, he looks physically exhausted.
Georgina nods. "Yeah, I was a bit worried about Zoltan as he went really quiet and weird for a while, was going to call the vet but he seemed alright when I finished work," she pauses, "early, I might add. You guys brought me here two hours before my shift ends. I better get paid 'til seven o'clock still."
"I'll have a word with your boss," Hippo reassures.
"You da man!" This time he accepts her high five.
"Right," Hardy murmurs, "I'll just read your statement back to you and you're free to go."

Chapter Seven

Frankie is fucked. Properly fucked.
His eyesight is the first thing he notices is fucked. He can't see colours properly, everything is black and white and pastel blues and yellows. Everything looks massive and everything is too loud. He's still in the kennels, in a different room to what he attacked the girl in and he can hear the cops somewhere close. Can hear the static on their radios, can hear them talking.
"Sick bastard gutted himself on top of her."
He can smell blood and the overpowering stench of other dogs.
"Oh fuck," he tries to say but his mouth is all wrong and all that comes out is a rumble like distant thunder and a strangled woof. I'm a fucking dog.
He forces himself off the floor and sees what life is like on four legs.

It's a peculiar sensation, like walking upright but on his hands and knees. Something tickles him at the base of his spine, he turns his new head to see what it is. I've got a tail. It sways back and forth and he seems to have zero control over it. What the fuck is that about?
The door opens and the girl walks in wearing green scrubs.
"What's all this racket about, Zoltan? I told you I'd come back for you."
I'll fucking well *Zoltan* you in a minute you fucking little cunt! His tail goes mental, his arse waggles ferociously.

Georgina crouches and reaches out to him. "Aw, did you miss me?"

No, I didn't fucking miss y—

She puts her hand on the back of his neck and kneads the muscles there and he instantly stops shouting. It feels so good.

"Aw, you is all tired and het up, aren't you?" She asks.

Frankie feels drool drip.

"You was a very brave boy earlier, yes you were, yes you were."

His tail will not shut the fuck up, he feels ninety percent tail.

Georgina rubs his neck and although he hates her with every fibre of his being he can't stop himself from rolling onto his back and sticking his legs in the air.

FRANKIE SAYS DIE

Chapter Eight

Tommy has drunk half a litre bottle of vodka but it hasn't taken the edge off his skull-splitting headache. He regrets telling Norman about his gift, regrets even having the bloody thing. He'd been boy wonder when he was with the circus as a kid, star of the fucking show. People queued for ages to get a reading off him once word got around but when puberty hit he started suffering for his ability.

His brain feels like it's a magma core which wants to explode from his eyes, ears and nose, the pressure is intolerable.

When he first began to suffer after readings the pain would knock him out for hours at a time. He stopped being useful, couldn't physically meet the public's demands, so he legged it.

He wants nothing more than to find a quiet cave, somewhere dark to squirrel away until this current bout of brain sickness passes but he needs more booze and more money to buy more booze. He squints at the passers-by, his pleas go mostly unheard, his squinting groggy state tutted at or ignored. They think he's like the others, a junkie, a user, but he hates the poison he has to ingest to take away the pain. He smiles when he sees what could be his saving grace.

Georgina.

She walks across the street with that silly little dog of hers. It goes everywhere with her, even work, a chocolate and caramel coloured dachshund called Zoltan. The sheriff badge tag on his little red collar reflects sunlight into Tommy's eyes and adds another level of pain.

Georgina gives him her pretty, but slightly manic, grin and pulls her chunky headphones around her neck. "Morning Thomas." She always calls him Thomas.

"Hey," he groans and hides the vodka amidst his blankets. He reaches forward to fuss the dog but he steps back and growls.

"Oh, don't mind him, he's just being a twat," Georgina crouches and massages the dog's neck. "He thinks he's a fucking hard man now."

"Oh?"

"Yeah, we've had an eventful night at the kennels, Zee was a proper Scooby Doo, only helped me apprehend a motherfucking serial killer."

"What the hell?" Tommy forces himself to sit up even though every movement makes his head pound.

Georgina tells him her abbreviated version of the night's events, an hour and a half later she notices Tommy's looking unwell.

"Migraine," he says when she asks and she rushes to the nearest Boots to get him some painkillers. She gives him a fiver too. She's a saint but when he lies down he notices Zoltan has pissed on his blankets.

The painkillers have finally started to take the edge off when he feels someone prod him in the stomach. Everything is still too bright when he opens his eyes and things get worse when he sees Digger and Screw hovering over him. Digger and Screw are other homeless people, he doesn't know why they're called those names. Digger is tall with dark, Romany features and has a look about him that's just inherently evil, like Damien Thorn grown-up.

FRANKIE SAYS DIE

Screw is an emaciated zombie, could be any age between twenty-five and fifty-five, covered in scars and only has one nostril due to excessive drug use.
"The high street is our patch," Screw says, his voice a nasal whine.
"We have told you." Digger sounds Eastern European.
"I'm just having a rest, I'm not asking for owt," Tommy moans, feebly hating the sound of his voice.
Digger crouches down and eyes the few meagre pence Tommy has collected in a coffee cup. "What the fuck's this then?"
"I never asked for it."
Digger empties the money into his hand. "What else you got?"
Tommy hesitates and Screw starts going through his pockets before he has a chance to do anything. His breath smells of decayed flesh.
Screw hands over the packet of painkillers and the five-pound note and grins when he finds the half bottle of vodka hidden beneath Tommy.
They take everything he's made that morning.
"The high street is ours," Digger says and nods to Screw.
Screw plants the toe of a filthy trainer in Tommy's face.
They walk off, soon lost amongst the pedestrians who steer clear of their type. Tommy takes a moment to get over the attack and then he begins to gather his blankets.

MATTHEW CASH

Chapter Nine

Well, it's the first time in his life he's ever been subservient to anyone. He yanks at the lead around his neck, another experience he could well do without and ignores Georgina's commands.
People are scary from ankle height, like walking trees, and there is so much stench everywhere. He can smell their feet, their crotches, arseholes and armpits. The most terrifying aspect of all of that is that the smells coming off Georgina make him feel safe, protected. He's Frankie fucking Foster, he shouldn't need to feel safe and protected, nothing should scare him. Sudden metallic thunder causes him to flinch and dart between Georgina's ankles and a shop front. The source of the sound is a roller shutter at the other end of the high street. It's so loud. Everyone's making so much noise, a thousand conversations simultaneously. This must be how some autistic people perceive the world. Jesus fucking Christ.

By the time they've walked up the High Street he's grateful for the dog lead and hates himself for it. This is bad. This is very bad. Frankie tries to focus on his history, the stuff he learnt, the magic. Knows there must be something he can do to get himself out of this hole he's in but his brain won't work properly. Everything's a distraction. One minute he's trying to remember how to project his soul temporarily without using the mantra and the next he seems to be possessed by his own nose, well the dog's nose, which is twitching and pulling like a dowser's rod or pendulum towards a fucking bakery. Frankie knows it's the dog's body, something is terribly wrong. Usually when taking over someone he just slides on in and shunts the other cunt out of their metaphorical chimney but this is the first time he's entered an animal and there's too much dog still left inside. He can see it, hear it, feel it. If he relaxes his concentration even slightly he starts having visions of stinky slippers and rubber toys. And every time he brushes against Georgina's feet he has the overwhelming desire to sniff them, lick them clean and it's not even sexual for once. Frankie tries to remind himself that he's the world's best serial killer, that he's been murdering people for the best part of five hundred years. He forces himself to concentrate on the six years he lived in Berlin after the war and became the Tiergarten Strangler, the string of prostitutes he left garrotted amongst the flowers, but then a flurry of snow walks past him and the doggybrain takes over and all he can think of is hard, rampant, fucking.

"Oh my God, I am so sorry!" Georgina cries and she sounds mortified. Frankie's head clears a little but all he can see is this fucking thing that looks like a cloud with legs. Something points in his saggy belly. He looks to the side and underneath himself and sees this thing that looks like a pink root of some description poking out near his hind legs. It drips onto the pavement.
An old lady pulls the cloud dog away from him and Frankie is almost certain it winks at him.
"Oh, poor, poor Mavis." The old lady tugs at the dog but it holds its ground.
"He's been neutered," Georgina says, still in apology mode.
"I don't care. You need to control your animal."

FRANKIE SAYS DIE

The white dog licks his face and is tugged viciously away as the old woman storms off.
"Looks like Mavis enjoyed it as much as he did," Georgina calls after her, but after she's out of hearing distance she crouches down and looks at him sternly. "What the fuck do you think you are doing? It's hardly consensual if you just run up and mount someone—"
Well, she didn't say 'no,' Frankie jokes but all that comes out is dog language.
"Don't you fucking talk back to me."
"—" he growls angrily.
And then she says something that completely floors him, it's the worst thing in the world, like being told you've got a month to live and they forgot to tell you three and a half weeks ago. Her index finger points down at him, it's like a lightning bolt from God Himself.
"BAD DOG!"
His legs buckle beneath him, his tail shoots between his back legs faster than he fucked the walking cloud, there isn't space for a thread of the finest gossamer between tail and butthole it is pressed so tightly. A dribble of piss turns into an epic golden lake below him and soaks his belly. He hangs his jowly head in shame, ears dangling in the urine. He is the saddest thing in the world, the universe even.
No! Frankie screams inside the stupid mutt's body but there's just too much dog left in there with him. He forces himself to take over the stupid stubby legs, determined that he's the alpha here, not some saggy-skinned, scrotum of a dog. He feels his essence flow throughout the ridiculous body, feels his power surge and grow. He roars and it comes from the bottom of his soul. Half a

millennium of sound and fury explodes from his mouth as a bark but it's not the bark of a dachshund it's the raucous cacophony a hellhound makes before it devours you whole, the heart-stopping ululation of the Black Shuck as it lowers its cyclopean head to snaffle up a newborn, it's the voice of Satan in dog form.

"No treat for you today, Zoltan Vickers," Georgina stands up and marches off.

Ha, fuck you and your tre— Frankie starts before remembering he's attached to a fucking lead.

Chapter Ten

Suki Matsugane thinks she only got the job at Mangalore because she's Japanese. Technically, she's as British as the girl outside the shop who looks like she's just stepped out of the Midsommar festival at Hälsingland. Suki's never even left the country, her mum was five when her grandparents moved to England and her father's from Birmingham, but it meets the shop's aesthetic and she has the credentials. She watches Georgina wrap Zee's lead around a lamppost and come in. "What's up, nerd?"
"Says the one coming into the comic book store."
Georgina leans on the counter and starts messing with the things on there.
Suki slaps at her hands. "You come in here to mess, or is there another reason?"
Georgina blows a strand of grey hair from her eyes. "Both?"
"Well, it shouldn't get busy 'til around eleven but Ken's out back so we can't stand around talking too obviously."
Georgina stands to attention and eyeballs the door marked staff. "You know he wants to jump your bones."
Suki's laugh fills the shop.
"It's true. I know these things, it's like extra-sensory perception," she pauses. "That, and the fact he can't take his eyes off of your tits."
"Jesus, George, have you come in here for any other reason other than to be lewd?"
"You know me–"
"So, that'll be a no then."

Georgina briefly flits in the direction of the manga books but gives up after three steps. "Is the new Junji Ito here yet?"

"Yeah, but it's not officially out for another week."

"You've read it haven't you?" Georgina squints with suspicion. The guilt must register on Suki's face as the Nordic-looking girl is agog. "I fucking knew it!"

"Look," Suki bends across the counter, her ample bosom making the eyes on her Pikachu hoody look more Minion than Pokémon. "I'll bring you a copy after my shift but you have to pay for it now."

Georgina jumps up and down excitedly and ferrets in her bag for her debit card. "You are the best friend a girl could have; do you know that?"

Suki nods and runs the transaction through the till with a smirk on her face. Her and Ken have been advance-selling copies of the new book since they came in.

Georgina tells her about the events of her night shift and as Suki's about to begin bombarding her with questions Ken comes onto the shopfloor and Georgina makes her excuses and leaves.

Georgina actually being the one to catch a possible serial killer well and truly trumps her getting advanced copies of their favourite manga novelist. Bitch.

Suki's obsessed with serial killers. A love for the macabre passed on from her grandmother and all the horrid little tales she used to tell her when she was little. Japanese folklore is full of sinister things that always scared her mother but excited her. Suki liked watching documentaries and reading books about serial killers, and wanted to know how their minds worked. The Smiler was one of the UK's

FRANKIE SAYS DIE

most infamous serial killers, one of the longest spanning too. She'd read books on how he had evaded capture since the late seventies, how his victims were left with the same, identical injuries, the Chelsea smile and the slit throat. Georgina said the guy was well old. Jesus, he'd have to be in his sixties at least. But the thing that shocked her, after the thought that Georgina could have been another Smiler victim, was how he ended his career. Why now? And why do that? Why cut off a piece of himself and try to force-feed it to someone? To kill yourself in such a way. That has to mean something somewhere to someone. It sounded like some kind of ritual.

Was it the fact that he was about to be caught, that finally, possibly due to old age, made him slip up and refuse to be taken alive?

So many unanswered questions.

Suki couldn't wait for her break so she could trawl Google. Georgina was so lucky.

"Urgh, that is so fucking gross," Suki sniggers and bites into her Subway, eyes glued to her phone. She's found an article all about ritual cannibalism and it's meaty to say the least. She's learnt all about rituals she never knew existed. The coolest being all about the Blessed Dead. How followers of certain holy people would grow psychoactive mushrooms on the bodies of their deceased shamans and priests and collect the liquified flesh to make holy oils. Sometimes they would suffocate sacrificial victims and seal all their orifices with wax to prevent leakage and speed up the liquefaction process. It was great lunchtime reading but she couldn't find anything about force-feeding people your own organs.

So, why did it ring a bell?

FRANKIE SAYS DIE

Chapter Eleven

Tommy checks the poster on the park gates for a second time to make sure his drink and drug-addled brain isn't playing tricks on him; it wouldn't be the first time and it won't be the last. The bright green font and the colourful imagery hurts his eyes but it's real enough. Greenfield's Circus is coming to town. He is shocked that the circus is still going after what happened with Jeremy Clifton. A chill runs through him and threatens to turn his already turbulent stomach.
Surely Ray Greenfield is dead by now.
No amount of intoxicating substances will block the memory of the seven shades of shit that the circus owner had beaten out of him when he found him after scarpering.

People used to run away to join the circus, Tommy ran away from it. They wanted him to stay, promised him regular powerful pharmaceuticals to quell the headfuckery that came after his readings, but he had seen so many friends and peers fall to drug usage that he was determined he wasn't going down that path.
He had been a kid.
The only time he drank alcohol was after a reading, and he only took painkillers sparingly, but it got to the stage, at several readings a day, when these things wouldn't touch the pain.
If Ray saw Tommy again he'd probably kill him, or worse, force him to come back and work at the circus again.

Regardless, he went into the park to find a quiet spot to ride out his headache. The circus wasn't due until the following weekend so there was plenty of time to make himself scarce.

Chapter Twelve

Georgina's parent's house is huge. She comes from money. The primary reason Frankie chose her to transfer into. The five-year plan after he takes over Georgina 's body involves investigating her whole family. See who was likely to be a problem. Then, bump the parents off in a car crash or something and get everything.
Once all that was safely achieved he could relax and partake in his favourite pastime - killing people.
This is just a temporary setback.

Being stuck in the mutt was completely fucking annoying and he didn't know what the fuck he was going to do other than keep a low profile until something came up. Although when Georgina unfastened his lead it took all his resolve not to bolt for the door.
The dog's sense of smell is extraordinary and Frankie uses it to his advantage, tracing where the dog normally navigates the house. Across a hallway, nose millimetres from the floor, he waddles into the kitchen and up to a row of food bowls. He's unbelievably thirsty and hungry, could murder a lager and a curry. Georgina opens the fridge, he catches a glimpse of beer cans in there, she takes out some juice, kicks off her shoes, walks through a huge lounge and crashes into the biggest armchair he's ever seen. He ignores the strange compulsion to run over and curl up against her and studies the water bowl. A fly performs a backstroke in it. He stares at Georgina and whines. Her headphones are

on and she's transfixed by a laptop screen. How the hell do dogs communicate with their owners? Lassie always managed to get her point across. Where was Doctor Dolittle when you needed him? Frankie lets the wide dog tongue fall into the water and pulls it back. This is going to take ages.

After he's managed to learn how to drink as a dog he sniffs at the dried food in the next bowl.

Unsurprisingly the dog food tastes like shit, it's no wonder pets are always begging for their humans' food. After he's forced himself to eat he finds he's naturally gravitating in the direction of Georgina. Before he knows it he's sitting on the carpet by her chair.

She pats the chair beside her butt and without any conscious control he's up there with her - well, after two attempts. They're drawn to each other like magnets - the dog and Georgina, and when Frankie relaxes his concentration just the slightest his inner pet takes over showing his natural love and loyalty for his owner. Frankie watches her scroll through her Facebook feed and feels drowsy after everything that's happened. He feels his eyes grow heavy and the dog part takes over to move into a more comfortable position. He lets it. With his face buried in the crotch of a twenty-two-year-old, something Frankie, in another body, would be incredibly excited about, he falls asleep and dreams about bones, walkies, stinky shoes and balls.

Frankie wakes up with a start and hopes it's all been a horrible nightmare. But it's real, he's still a stupid dog. Georgina's vanished but her laptop is still switched on on the armchair.

FRANKIE SAYS DIE

If only I had the dexterity to use that keyboard. There must be something on the internet which can help me.
He tries to remember his repertoire of incantations and mantras, the large array of magic he learnt in his fifty-odd years as a warlock, before the secret to his immortality was revealed, but it's like the doggy mind is growing, the host trying to reject him. His memory is shrinking. Is it to do with the differences between the brains of humans and dogs? He has to do something that's pure Frankie, he knows that much. Maybe he can shock the dog out of him completely so he can at least have one hundred percent control. He needs to kill someone.

The most important things about the perfect murder are planning and preparation, these things go straight out of the cat flap though when you're a homicidal hound. Sure, you can tail your next victim if you've got a nose for such things. Maybe if you're a Saint Bernard or one of those massive things that resemble a dog that's fucked a lion you could possibly eat your victim afterwards but when you're a dachshund you're limited in both execution and disposal. Tricky. But Frankie is an expert at killing and has gotten away with it for five hundred years. It doesn't matter if it looks like murder just as long as he gets the buzz he needs.

Frankie has spent the afternoon whilst Georgina's been asleep observing her mum and dad. He's decided that he likes them a lot more than Georgina, they literally shower him in treats and even share what food they're eating, especially if he stares at them in a special way and cocks his head on one side to let one of his ears flop. Her Dad even put some lager in a bowl for him when he worked the doggy magic. It's because of this Frankie decides to kill Georgina's mum first.

FRANKIE SAYS DIE

Chapter Thirteen

Frankie sprawls across the sofa, tired from just walking back and forth to the water bowl. Georgina's mum strokes his head and sings her own dog-inspired version of the Ramones' *Baby I Love You*. It's embarrassing as fuck but he can feel himself falling asleep, yet again. He shakes his head, those ears flap about like it's some kind of defence mechanism.

"Aw, what's up Zee?" Georgina's mum and dad laugh way too long every time they say this. "Whassa matter my ickle doggo?" Mum says and her fingers move towards the back of his neck.

No, Frankie slides off the sofa, don't you fucking dare touch that, bitch. I'm done sleeping. He runs as quickly as Zoltan's silly, stubby legs will take him, out of the lounge and across the kitchen tiles.

He takes a few moments to peruse the layout of the room before pulling open one of the drawers with his mouth. Okay, let's shake things up a little. He lowers his belly to the floor and releases a piss that seems never-ending. It's quite remarkable how much urine the dog's bladder holds and how frequently it needs to empty it. He patters over to the back door, emits a high-pitched whelp that he hopes sounds like a dog in distress, drops onto his side, flops his tongue out and closes his eyes. He hears the rush of feet.

"Oh my God, Zee!"

He cracks open an eye just in time to see her slip in the piddle puddle, her bare feet fly up in the air as she falls

and he hears the crash of her head hitting the open drawer. She yells in pain and he's up and on her immediately. "Zee, not now," she slurs with dizziness. He scrabbles along her chest towards her face, a quick scan inside the bottom drawer tells him there's nothing in there that would aid the dog him in her murder. Shit.
There's blood spotting the floor where she banged her head but it's not enough.
Shit.
Improvisation was usually one of his strong points but this body was so limiting.
Shit. Shit. Shit.
He wondered briefly whether he could rip her throat out with his teeth or whether she would just lift him off her before he had a chance. Her arms flap at her sides, she's still stunned by the fall.
Come on, Frankie boy. Shit.
Then the lightbulb moment happens.
He twists around and clamps his jaws down hard on her left tit. When she opens her mouth to scream at the new level of pain he presses his sphincter down and squeezes with all his might.
It feels like the whole universe is shooting out of his arsehole, within seconds her horrified screaming transcends into thick suffocating chokes. The whole kitchen smells like onions, chicken and shit. Frankie bites harder and forces everything out. Blood fills his mouth and her floppy boob pops out of her ripped top. Her hands flap around trying to grab for him. He turns to see the damage. Mum's mouth is an erupting volcano of mince and meatballs, thick, rich brown blocks her nostrils and covers her face. He sees a vein throbbing in her neck and digs at it as fast as he can with his front paws. Within seconds he's

FRANKIE SAYS DIE

struck oil and her jugular sprays across the white ceiling and up the walls.
After what seems like an eternity she stops moving. He's covered in shit and blood, not normally a problem, he's bathed in worse stuff than that in his time but he knows that he's gotta make like the littlest hobo and move on. Adrenaline gives him the rush he requires and he's more in charge than he's ever been. He jumps up on to the open drawer, opens the next, jumps up and does the same with the one above until he's up on to the work surface. He leaves bloody, shitty pawprints as he runs across cutting boards and ceramic hotplates towards the open kitchen window.
The fall looks a long way but it's grass.
Fuck it.
He falls out of the window, nothing graceful at all in his landing but luckily he isn't hurt in the fall.
I'm free.
He has no idea where he's going but he'll figure that out once he gets there.
In the house Georgina shrieks.

MATTHEW CASH

Chapter Fourteen

Tommy's just woken up beneath a tree in the park when he sees the dachshund walk past. It looks like Georgina's dog. It's not on a lead and there doesn't appear to be anyone else with it. He sits up and calls the dog's name but it ignores him and carries on. It's a mess, covered in filth and what looks like blood. Tommy watches it crawl down a muddy incline and slop into a stream. The dog has a red collar with a sheriff badge tag on it. It is Zoltan. He doesn't want to scare the thing away; he creeps toward the stream dreading finding out what the hell has happened to cause the dog to be in such a state.

The dog submerges itself in the water to clean off the filth on its body. It rubs its fur against the smooth rocks until it's clean and then starts rolling in the grass to dry itself off. Tommy finds it remarkable how intelligent the animal is. He gets closer until he's within arm's reach and says the dog's name again. It spots him and lets out a hollow growl but before it has a chance to run Tommy grabs hold of its collar. Zoltan is a rabid flurry of tooth and claw, but he's also a dachshund. Tommy picks him up and holds him away from his body. The little dog twists and bucks but can't get free of his grasp, his short legs are useless, all he can do is snap and growl in the air.

"Hey, Zee, it's me, you know me. What's got into you? Where's Georgina?"

Zoltan ejects a stream of hot urine in Tommy's face. His instinct is to yell and he gets a mouthful before he clamps his lips together and lowers the pissing dog.

MATTHEW CASH
"What the hell is up with you? Why are you so scared?"
The fear that something may have happened to Georgina makes him decide to read Zoltan. He's never read an animal before but he needs to know why the little dog is so anxious and on its own. He hopes it won't hurt as much as it does with people.
Tommy refuses to let go of Zoltan, he closes his eyes and lets his gift take over.
Blood. Bodies. So many bodies.
Thousands of corpses crowd inside his head. There are victims of every kind of death here, of every age.
Tommy quits using his power. For the first time ever it must be wrong. Why would this be in a dog's mind or future? He tries again.
There's a man with long grey hair and a beard. His face is scarred with what look like runic symbols that have been carved into the skin. He's dressed like he's Shakespeare or someone, billowing sleeves, high collar. His eyes are unnaturally grey, almost white and they stare straight at Tommy, even though that's impossible.

Tommy tries to withdraw from this bizarre ordeal but can't, it's like something else has got a hold of him psychically.
"Oh, this could be most useful," says the man with the grey eyes.
There's an invisible hand clamped around his brain, probing parts he never knew existed. Tommy doesn't know who's reading who and he can't break the hold it has over him.
"Who the hell are you?" Tommy manages to splutter.
The man with the grey eyes smiles, some of the nastiest teeth Tommy's ever seen, even on the homeless circuit.

FRANKIE SAYS DIE

The dachshund's hot body is a deadweight in his hands, he can't see it but he can feel it. It's not moving.
"What's going on?" Tommy asks again.
"I'm a five-hundred-year-old warlock who goes by many names, but you can call me Frankie."
"What are you doing in my friend's dog?"
"A little mishap but that's where you can help me."
"I... How?"
"Oh, it's quite simple. All you have to do is learn some magic words and make your friend eat the dog's liver."
"This is insane. I'm not doing anything of the sort."
"Oh, you will. Now we've established this link I have many ways of persuading you."
"No, I'm no—"
The warlock laughs and it feels like Tommy's brain is on fire. Electric shocks zap through his head, with each one he feels every nerve in his body twitch and burn. There's acid in his veins. His vision blackens and his limbs go stiff like he's having a grand mal seizure. He feels the dachshund drop from his grasp and then there's nothing.

Tommy doesn't know how long he's been unconscious but when he wakes up he feels euphoric. All his senses are in overdrive, he's never felt so amazing. His automatic response to this is that someone has spiked him with something. It isn't right. Sure, the sun is shining down on him and all his aches and pains have gone but he feels vibrant, strong and there's no reason for him to feel vibrant and strong. He sits up and it takes all of his will power not to jump to his feet and start dancing around. Zoltan is lying on the grass beside him asleep. Tommy remembers

what he hopes was delusion, madness or a dream. It has to be one of those things. Has to be. Zoltan yawns, stretches his long body, wags his tail excitedly and raises one of his baked bean shaped eyebrows at him. *Oh good, you're awake.* Zoltan's mouth doesn't move at all, the warlock's voice is just there in his head.
"I'm going insane."
The dog walks around him in a slow circle.
If only things were that simple.
Tommy ignores Zoltan and despite feeling great knows the truth of the matter. Too much time on the streets, too much booze, too much of everything. This was his call to seek help. "I need to get you back to Georgina."
I shat in her mum's mouth.
"Course you did, dog, course you did." Tommy scoops the dog up under one arm and walks away from his resting place.
I do have legs.
"I'm not going to respond to you. I know I'm going crazy, no one else has to know just yet."
Zoltan growls like a hellhound.
"BAD DOG!"
Fuck you.

Chapter Fifteen

It's the overflowing mountain of shit in numerous consistencies, the mouthful of mince with added goujons that makes her puke harder than she's ever puked in her life. It feels like her stomach is actually going to prolapse from her mouth inside out and slap on top of the heap of regurgitation like a misshaped fish. The blood isn't as bad as the shit, ridiculously enough, even though in this instance it means what appears to be the death of her mother. It's the mouth. Full. Of. Shit. Georgina notices twin trails of brown syrup running from her mum's nostrils running down over her cheeks and heaves herself raw.
"Mum?" she says stupidly, like her mum would just lay there with her throat in ruins and a mouth full of faeces if she was in any way alive. The only sign that anyone else has been in the kitchen are shitty bloody paw prints and the open drawers. "Zee!" she calls, immediately thinking whoever did this took her dog. She sees the pawprints lead across the work surface towards the open window and gasps. Zoltan went after mum's killer!
Georgina has watched enough television, read enough books, to know not to touch anything. It's obvious the perpetrator came in through the back door, her parents always left it unlocked if there was someone in the house, and if she touched or moved anything she would likely be tampering with evidence.
She rushes to find the number Hippo and Hardy gave her even though there's no way her mother's murder can be

anyway connected. Unless The Smiler was part of some top-secret organisation, or had helpers like the guy in Saw.

The cops come but it's not her mates Hippo and Hardy. The first thing they want to know is where her dad was.
"Oh my God, do you think he did this?" Georgina's brain is going haywire.
"We didn't say that, Miss," a lady police officer tells her but her overactive imagination has taken a high-speed train and is miles away.
"I mean, they aren't that old, they still have sex and stuff. Maybe this was a weird sex game that went wrong, I mean everyone has their fetishes and who am I to criticise what floats my parents' boats, I mean for a while, when I was nineteen, I was really obsessed with women's feet, like *really* obsessed, not skanky crusty old ones with toenails like pork scratchings mind, pretty feet, but there was a time when I worked at Hoofs shoe shop in town and I'd help all these other girls try on high heels and stuff and as soon as I got home I'd have to masturbate until my clit was sore and my fingers were numb but—"
"Miss Vickers," the police officer interrupts, "stop. You're obviously in shock."
Georgina nods, the officer is probably right, a flash of her getting the sack after they found the stash of inner soles she'd snuck from people's shoes in her locker plays back and she feels herself flush.
"No, I doubt this was a sex game," she says dreamily, "my dad was always squeamish when it came to poo."
"Does your father have a number we can contact him on?"
"Yeah, but he always leaves his phone here." She scours the kitchen and points to the fruit bowl where a smartphone

rests like a banana. "He's always harping on about coping for twenty-seven years without one."
"Okay, well all we can do is let the forensics do their job and wait for your father to come home." The police officer leads her into the lounge, away from the crime scene and all those investigating it. "Do you have anyone who can come and sit with you?"

"And you say her mouth was full of shit?" Suki desperately wants to take a peek in the kitchen but it's totally out of bounds.
Typical. My first actual, real life murder scene and I can't bloody well see a thing.
Georgina nods slowly. She's a numb and hollow thing at the moment. Her mum has been murdered but the absurdity of the shit part has made it more surreal and unbelievable than it would be if it was your generic, run-of-the-mill murder.
"Why the shit?" Suki asks, her little nose crinkles like she can smell the stuff.
Georgina shrugs.
"Obviously the killer wanted to humiliate your mum before he, or she, did the deed," Suki continues, lacking any kind of sensitivity.
"Mmhmm."
"And the cops think your dad did it, don't they?"
Georgina shakes herself back to reality. "They've not actually said that."
"Yeah, but… Did your parents fight a lot?"
"No, hardly ever. Well, not in front of me."

MATTHEW CASH

Suki has an image of her friend's parents arguing, the fight becoming physical and her dad shouting something along the lines of, "I've had enough of your shit. So have some of mine." She decides it's probably best not to share this vision with Georgina. Not just yet. "Sometimes people just flip," Suki pauses and tries everything in her willpower to stop herself from saying it but out it comes regardless. "Sometimes people… just… lose… their… shit!"

Georgina's glare is almost radioactive. It's a good job they know each other inside out, know that their collective depravity is just a defence mechanism against their real emotions. Suki decides to change tactics. "I brought you the new Ito." She gives her a small dark beige hardback book covered in morbid gold scribbles and a girl's frightened eyes.

Georgina manages a half-smile. "Kind of coincidental that the cover is brown."

FRANKIE SAYS DIE

Chapter Sixteen

Tommy doesn't know where Georgina lives but he knows where she works so as he circumnavigates the park lake he heads toward the exit closest to the kennels. At least they would be able to hold Zoltan safely and contact Georgina. The dog is persistent, struggling beneath his arm. He's nearly dropped it twice, and it's still talking to him too.
Let me go you fucking tramp!
Tommy ignores the voice; he'll go to one of the hostels after the dog is safe and ask for help. It's no surprise to him that something like this has surfaced in him with all the pressures he had when younger but he clings to the hope that the simple fact he's lucid about the whole thing is a good sign. He's relieved, relieved that something has finally happened to make him act upon his situation and take the first step in trying to build himself a life. His unfaltering optimism is even stronger after his epiphany beneath the tree.
He quickens his step as the exit comes into view and doesn't even pause when he sees two familiar faces slouch through the park gates, Digger and Screw. He's not in their territory, they should leave him alone.
Tommy thinks he's going to just be ignored, which is always the better option, especially as they've beaten the crap out of him already today but he's not that lucky.
"Where did you get that?" Digger demands stepping in his path, eyes black holes to a galaxy nobody wants to explore.

MATTHEW CASH

"It's my friend's," Tommy says and tries to walk around them.

Why are you shitting yourself about them two? Zoltan laughs in his head and then without Tommy having any control a montage of Digger and Screw's greatest hits, and kicks, pop up in his memory.

Pff, they're just school bullies. Fucking fight back you soppy cunt. They'll leave you alone then.

"I bet he's nicked it to try and get more sympathy from the park dwellers, Dig." Screw nudges the other man, "Think about it. All these cunts walking through here with their mutts. Gonna feel sorry for a soft cunt like him with a cute little dog. He can play the whole 'he's my only friend' bollocks."

Digger's eyes seem to blacken even more with what his sidekick has suggested.

"Give us the dog!" the dark-haired man shouts.

Screw nods and grins toothless, he looks like a pottery project gone wrong. "'s got a tag too, Dig. Might be a reward."

The ghost of a smile appears on Digger. "That's what it is. Get the dog Screw."

Don't you give me to them cunts, Zoltan growls beneath Tommy's arm.

"I won't, don't worry," Tommy replies and instantly regrets talking aloud to the animal.

Screw reaches for the dachshund and Tommy jumps back a few steps. Both men step forward, Digger grabs a handful of Tommy's hair. "Give us the fucking dog."

Zoltan's jaws snap and Screw almost gets his fingers bitten off. "Fucking little shit."

Digger pulls his fist back ready to strike Tommy and Zoltan goes stiff under his arm.

FRANKIE SAYS DIE

Oh, fuck this for a game of soldiers.

Chapter Seventeen

Frankie slips into Tommy's body with ease and congratulates himself for his wise thinking early on whilst the tramp was unconscious and trying him on for size then. It's been a few centuries since he took over someone psychically, it's nowhere near as good, or permanent, as following the rules of the ritual and there's the added danger of the body his actual soul is in being at risk whilst he's doing it. Nevertheless, Frankie, now behind Tommy's eyes, drops the sausage dog, ducks Digger's fist and thrusts his index and middle fingers into his very prominent Adam's apple. Digger recoils, eyes wide, as he starts choking. Before Screw can even acknowledge that Tommy has seemingly struck back Frankie shoves the same two fingers up the singular nostril of his burnt-out coke nose and pulls him into a headbutt that destroys the rest of it. He steps back to take a breather, impressed with how healthy and agile Tommy's body is for someone homeless. Whilst Digger paws at his throat and Screw stares cross-eyed at his nasal explosion Frankie stoops to pick up Zoltan's floppy body, lays him gently on a nearby bench before turning back to the two men. He takes a moment to think about what he's going to do with them, never one to miss the opportunity to kill or maim, he quickly scans the surrounding area for things he can use. This could be the start of a new and interesting era. The two men begin to recover from their injuries. Frankie daydreams about what serial killer is about to be born.

MATTHEW CASH

They lunge for him just as he makes his mind up that the next phase in his legacy will be outdoor related murder, possibly specifically parks.

Frankie crouches as they pounce, picks up the twig he eyed a few seconds before, jams it into the bloody hole on Screw's face, grabs Digger by the ears and, using the man's own momentum, pulls his head down hard toward the railings by the lake. A rusty green spike bursts out of the back of Digger's head and Frankie stands back and laughs as both men dance funny little death jigs.

FRANKIE SAYS DIE

Chapter Eighteen

Tommy's eyes spring open. There's a lot to take in. Screw looks like a real-life Pinocchio, there's a stick protruding from his face and he's doing the Pentozali except he's not Greek and there are definitely no plates to smash. Digger is impaled on the lake fence, arms going up and down like he's trying to take off. Zoltan woofs excitedly and runs rings around Screw's unsteady feet until he trips over and faceplants the ground. He crunches when he lands and the piece of wood pops through the top of his head and knocks his filthy baseball cap off.

Tommy's lost for words and when they do come out they don't really make an awful lot of sense. Zoltan stops at his feet and barks a few times, the little dog's bark sounds way bigger than his breed. As the noise of his cries reach Tommy's ears they're translated inside his head as the voice of the warlock.

You can't let those fuckers boss us around.

Tommy stares down in horror at the dachshund. "Us?"

Look, you can believe this is all a figment of your imagination for as much as you want but I am in control.

Panic sets in and Tommy scans the area for witnesses. There's no one in sight so he runs towards the exit.

Wait. Aren't you going to take me back to my owner?

Tommy ignores the voice in his head. To hell with the fucking dog. It's probably microchipped anyway, someone else can hand him in.

MATTHEW CASH

Cars whiz past on the busy main road and he can't help but worry about the dog getting hit by a vehicle.

I wonder how much mess it will make? I'll turn from sausage into burger.

Further proof that the voice is a part of me, Tommy thinks, but then another part of him questions how come he can fully embrace his own psychic powers and dismiss any others. Zoltan is right behind him, stupid-ass grin, tail wagging furiously.

"If you're what you say you are, how did you end up in her dog?"

An accident. For some reason, the first bloody time ever too, when I started saying the mantra that would enable my soul to transfer to Georgina, she wasn't totally under my command and her dog got in the way.

Tommy laughs humourlessly. They walk alongside the main road; he notices the dog's remarkable road sense and how his actions seem a lot more controlled than how the dog usually acts; like his legs are all trying to run in separate directions.

"If this is true and I'm not going insane then why the hell should I help you transfer yourself into a perfectly innocent young girl?"

You've not really got a lot of choice, son, the warlock tells him. *I can pretty much take over your body whenever I want to.*

"So, take me instead."

Aw, that's very noble of you chap but no, a ripe, young twenty-something girl is a better option than some skinny-arse, smelly vagrant.

Tommy stops. "If you can possess me whenever you like then why don't you just do it until you find her again?"

Zoltan turns away towards the traffic. *Smart arse, aren't you? It ain't that fucking simple, is it? You think if I could do*

FRANKIE SAYS DIE

that I would be fannying around stuffed up a dachshund's arse? Well?

Tommy shrugs.

The fucking answer is no, boy, no. I can temporarily manipulate your body, yeah. But it's like a car rental or something when you've still got all the fucking company stickers on the doors and shit, I can't make you completely mine.

"You did a pretty good job back there for fuck's sake. My fingerprints and everything are going to be all over them pair."

Ah, but I didn't talk to them, did I?

"How the fuck should I know? I was just ejected out of the speeding car like something out of a James Bond fi… wait," Tommy can't stop the grin. "You can't talk through me unless you've fully transferred yourself, right?"

Bingo.

Laughter takes control of him. "So, that's why you need me. To say your magic words for you because I'm the only one who can help you?"

You're gifted in more ways than one.

"Was that sarcasm?"

Woof.

Tommy smiles triumphantly at the dog. "Well, good luck with that then, cuz I'm not helping you, no matter what."

You don't have a choice.

"But I do."

Fuck. Zoltan paces back and forth. *How about if I teach you how to do it?*

"How to do what?"

Transfer yourself into another body. Think about it, you could find someone mega-rich.

"But surely you'll already be teaching me this by getting me to recite your words?"

Zoltan growls and bares his teeth. *You're a cunt.*

Tommy's smug now. "I'm sorry but I'm not helping you possess my friend. You say you're five hundred years old? Well, you've had more than enough time. I'm not helping you."

You will. You'll be begging to get me out of your head when you see what I can do. Those two twats in the park deserved everything they got. Well wait until you come round to the bodies of innocent people. Women. Children. I'm a fucking curse on Mankind, the Grim fucking Reaper. I was Jack the Ripper, Fred West and some you've never even heard of. I'll make you fucking famous, son, a household name. They'll make books and films showing the evil shit that you will do, not me, oh no, I've never been convicted for a crime. It's always the hosts they blame. Nothing can stop me and nothing can contain me. I'll always find a way out.

"You'll still be trapped in the body of a stupid dachshund though," Tommy squeaks.

Ha, you think you're the only one with a gift like yours? Poppycock. I'll find another psychic.

"That's if that body lasts long enough."

The dog backs away a step but then laughter sounds in Tommy's head. *Was that an actual threat? Oh my God.*

Tommy can't keep the sadness from his face. "Zoltan is terminally ill. It's the main reason Georgina is allowed to take him to work with her and doesn't let him out of her sight."

Chapter Nineteen

"So, don't they come with, like, GPS now or something?" Suki says as they leave Georgina's house.
Georgina's dad came back and the police wanted to talk to him on their own so the two girls went out to look for Zoltan.
"Seriously?" Georgina really doesn't know if Suki is being genuine or not.
"I mean, yeah. Why not? You see all this stuff in the old James Bond films, surely if they can whack all that info on a microchip they can have some kind of tracking device too. You could have a little app on your phone to find him and everything."
"That's a pretty good idea but I don't think the technology is available right now."
"Bollocks. They can put it in phones and stuff."
"I did think about getting him a GPS tracking *collar* but I hardly ever let him off the lead and even if I do he just stands there like I'm trying to abandon him. He likes his lead, makes him feel safe having me to hide behind."
Zoltan really wasn't adventurous, he spent almost all of his time lying around sleeping, or thinking about sleeping. The most exertion he usually took part in was finding things to cover himself with, like blankets, freshly laundered clothes, food, his own urine, and walking to the bus stop. It was only because he had been off his food the previous year that Georgina realised anything was wrong with him.

MATTHEW CASH

"He's been acting like a dickhead since the incident at the kennels."

"What do you mean?"

"Well, he was aggressive towards Tommy."

"Tommy the tramp?"

"Don't call him that!"

"But he is one."

"He's homeless and a really nice guy I'll have you know." Georgina points towards the council estate, Zoltan's lead jangles in her hand.

"Would you?" Suki asks, nudging her friend with her shoulder.

"Would I what?"

Suki smirks. "You know. Would you…" she makes a series of clicks and a two-toned whistle before making a circle out of her thumb and forefinger and poking the hole with her other index finger.

Georgina screws her face up in disgust. "Well, yeah, probably. He's very attractive but I'd, like, want some reassurance, about, you know…"

"That he wasn't an *actual* dirty tramp?"

Georgina grimaces but nods.

She's taking Suki the way she always walks with Zoltan to get the bus. They always get on the bus at the same stop whether she's going to work or taking him to the vets for his monthly check-up and to get his painkillers. She hopes he'll stick to what he knows and not go far. In fact she knows he can't walk that far, he's old and his arthritic joints won't let him. She's actually amazed at the feat of endurance in successfully climbing out of the kitchen window and jumping the four feet to the ground. Dachshunds are not climbers and they are most definitely not jumpers, or landers, and normally Zee was pretty crap

FRANKIE SAYS DIE

at just walking. But something had kicked in when her mum got killed and she was petrified, but equally proud, that her little dude had heroically braved the pain and given chase. Even though it was completely out of character. Usually, unless he really knew someone, he would cower behind her legs and piss himself or bark loud enough to wake the dead. People, who heard his woof before seeing what breed he was, often thought he was a bigger dog, like a Doberman or rottweiler and she knew, deep down, Zoltan thought he was too. But he was a coward, would only go after other dogs when they were at a safe enough distance, hated going outside if there was any kind of weather more adverse than overcast, and was allergic to grass. He was not the sort of dog to leap out of kitchen windows to face down a fucking murderer.

"I think maybe seeing me in danger might have broken him a bit mentally," Georgina thinks aloud.

"And when he saw your mum attacked he just flipped his wig, lost his shit, and went after them like a badass Scooby?"

"Maybe."

As they stand by the bus stop a lorry crawls past them, a red and green tent gaily painted on its storage container. Signage tells them that Greenfield's Circus is one of a kind.

"That tent looks like Freddy Krueger." Suki kicks at junk on the pavement.

"We should go and check the park. Where that truck is no doubt going."

"Since when did you ever take Zee to the park? You said last time you took him to the park a mallard tried rape him."

Georgina laughs hard at that; she'd forgotten all about the time Zee interrupted what can only be described as a duck gangbang and how a horny duck actually mounted him and kept chasing him with its breasts fluffed up and wings beating like mad. It was hilarious.

"I've still got the video," she says through tears. "It's got ten thousand views on TikTok."

"So, you reckon there's a chance he's hit the park for some duck action, like he's got his own little doggie bucket list and he's trying to tick things off?"

"With how he's acted today nothing would surprise me."

Chapter Twenty

Ray Greenfield's armchair is bolted to the floor of the storage unit. Opposite is its twin. In the twin sits an old man with a drooping white moustache. He clutches the handle of a shopping trolley emblazoned with words such as Megadeth, Iron Maiden, Guns 'n' Roses and The Spice Girls like its contents are more precious than the Ark of the Covenant. He sniffs up a sliver snot-trail and stares around the unit's interior. It's decked out like an elaborate lounge, a three piece black leather suite, mahogany book cases filled with tomes of all ages and sizes, even a bar.
"You wouldn't know this was all on the back of a lorry going at God knows how many miles an hour, would you?" Norman says and reaches for the small glass of sherry that sits on a table between them next to a silver bell.
Ray Greenfield is a hulk of a man, six and a half feet tall with a fifty-two inch chest. When he took over the circus, thirty years ago, he was the strongman, although he doesn't perform as that now he's almost a match for their current one. His fingers are thick with silver rings, some are pointed and completely cover the digits, tattoos cover most exposed skin. With long, greying black hair and a beard to match he casts a formidable figure, like a cross between Ozzy Osbourne and Rob Zombie but only if they had spent twenty years on steroids. A streak of pure white runs through his hair just above his right eye which has the reddish hue of albinism to its pupil. He likes to tell people who are brave enough to ask about this freakish

abnormality that it's where God tried to strike him down. He smiles at Norman and takes pleasure as the geriatric trembles slightly at his full set of silver capped teeth.

"They're new," Norman says pretending all is well.

"I'm glad you like my quarters," Ray says waving a hand around him. "I like to call it my road abode."

"Oh, ha, very good."

"I hear you've been liaising with someone of interest to me," Ray says, casually picking fluff off the cuff of his green ringmaster jacket.

Norman sips his sherry and nods eagerly. "I've been talking to Tommy for around a year. He's a good lad."

"That he is, that he is," Ray sighs. "I just wish he'd come back to us under his own will."

"The readings make him really ill," Norman wags a finger at his temples. "I think they give him headaches. Migraines."

Ray remembers how ill the readings made Tommy, remembers the screaming, the tearing of hair, the smashing of his head against the walls to try and knock himself unconscious. "There are plenty of ways to counteract the effects of these things nowadays."

"Of course, of course," Norman starts, "but why would you voluntarily put yourself through that pain?"

"Money," Ray chuckles, "and power."

Norman has nothing worthwhile to add so he drinks the remainder of his sherry.

"Do you know, I have the sight too?"

Norman looks surprised. "Well, why do you need two of you?"

Ray points a steel-tipped fingertip at his red pupil. "I only see the past, he sees the future."

FRANKIE SAYS DIE

It's Norman's turn to laugh now. "Everyone sees the past. It's already happened, ain't it?"

Ray can't be bothered to explain that he means that through that unholy red eye of his he sees dead people, the memories of people still trapped inside the living. He closes his normal eye and sees the three women crowding behind Norman, ropes, blue fluorescent umbilicals, sprout from their translucent bosom and penetrate Norman's skull and chest. They're a medley of different ages and styles, the youngest is in her early twenties and dressed in fashions of the forties, fifties, the others are older and in more recent garb. They're old lovers, girlfriends, wives, those he still cares deeply about and can't let go. Ray sees these spectres floating above and behind people like man-shaped balloons. He doesn't know if they're actually the souls of the dead or a projection of the living person's mind.

"Nevertheless my dear friend you have found my lost boy and for that I am very grateful," Ray lifts a silver hip flask up and shows it to Norman. "How much time do you want now? Ten? Fifteen?"

Norman's eyes light up behind his glasses. "Well, I've met a new lady…" Behind him the ghosts of his past conquests roll their eyes in unison. "She's younger than me too."

"But you have to remember, Norman, I can't turn back time, I can only promise you extra. What if you get ill? In body or of mind? You know once this is set nothing will be able to change it, not illness or suicide."

Norman pales, contemplates Ray's words, then blurts out,"Twenty! I want twenty years." The oldest of his spirits laughs silently and shakes her head.

MATTHEW CASH

"You really want to keep going until your eighty-nine?" Ray says in disbelief.

"I'd go on forever if there was a way," Norman spits stubbornly clutching the handles of the shopping trolley until his knuckles crack.

"Very well," Ray leans across and hands Norman the silver flask. "Drink it all down in one, no questions asked, just like you did in 1983."

Norman snatches the flask and unscrews the cap, a ghostly waft of white vapour curls up from out of the flask. He presses the cold metal against his mouth and drinks greedily. When he brings the bottle down his lips are slick with a silver liquid.

"Let's drop you off then," Ray says, reaching across to retrieve the flask. As he does so he plucks the silver bell from the table between thumb and forefinger and rings it. Norman looks around expectantly and then in a rush he, the shopping trolley and the armchair have vanished into a hole in the floor, his ghosts rushing along with him like they're on bungee cords.

Ray laughs and looks forward to reading about the strange accident that will no doubt appear in the local newspapers. Pensioner in armchair in traffic collision.

Chapter Twenty-One

Frankie is angry. It's been a long, long time since he was in a pickle as bad as this. Last time he remembers anything as close as risky as the fix he is in now was on his third transfer. Things were a lot harder then anyway, especially when it came to matters medical.

He had stalked a yeoman in the Norfolk countryside for several months, making mental notes of his place of power and how much land he owned, checking that he was young and able-bodied but didn't count on underlying health issues. He only had to take in a few breaths with the new body's lungs to know something wasn't right. Luckily, in situations like that, he would, if necessary, swap bodies more regularly until he found one of his liking but none of the bloody people he took over were mute or a different species.

He recalled seeing a dog on BBC's That's Life that sounded like it could say 'sausages', he forgets what its name was, Esther Rantzen or something, but knows the chances of training the dog's voice box to talk are slim, especially in the little time he has left.

Just my fucking luck that I meet a fucking psychic who has no will to live.

"You think I haven't got the will to live?" Tommy gasps. "If I hadn't got the will to live I'd be dead already or like that pair you just saw off."

They walk alongside boarded up pubs and shops, Tommy can never remember them ever being open.

Help me then.

MATTHEW CASH

"You've said that you are a body-swapping, serial-killing, warlock who has been around for five hundred years and, as a hobby, you continuously reinvent yourself, quite literally, as a different mass murderer when you see fit."
It's a good job dogs can't smile because I'd probably look like a right smug bastard now.
"I'm not letting you hurt Georgina. There must be something else we can do. I mean if you're as powerful as you let on, why can't you just bloody well think of something?"
He's right, Frankie knows he is but there's no way he can remember even half the shit that he learnt five hundred years ago. If only he had thought about what he was doing all those lifetimes ago, preserved some of his spell books.
I don't suppose you know of any present day witches or warlocks, do you?
Tommy's face goes grey for a moment.
You do, don't you?
"There was a woman who reckoned she was a witch that used to ride with Greenfield's but she's got to be dead by now."
You'd be surprised. We can be resilient fuckers. Frankie trawls his memory for any spells or incantations that could manipulate or change animals. Maybe if he could transform into a parrot he could get the chant out, although there would still be the issue of the liver-eating. Anger boils inside of him, this puny mortal is getting on his tits big time. He hasn't got a clue where Tommy is taking him but the streets have turned residential. Across the road a young mother carries groceries towards a newly built house.
Okay, he says to Tommy, *let's see how much of this you can handle before you change your mind.*

FRANKIE SAYS DIE

"No!" Tommy cries out as Zoltan runs across the road and up to the woman taking bags from a car boot.

MATTHEW CASH

Chapter Twenty-Two

Norman doesn't know what happened but he feels every second of it. Every part of him screams with pain and he's lying in the middle of the road. Two blurry figures rush towards him.
"Fucking hell!" one says and crouches down to him, it's a young girl with grey hair.
Her friend comes into view, mobile phone in hand. "Why is there an armchair?"
"Now is not the time to question things, Suki," the grey haired girl says. "I'm trying to remember my first aid."
"I think I'll be alright," Norman tries to sound as cheerful as he can. He doesn't feel too bad, only a few scrapes and bruises. Ray's special elixir will see to that.
"Umm—" the grey haired girl starts nervously.
"You're fucking legs are pointing the wrong way, dude!" her mate finishes.
"Oh," Norman says and sees the higgledy-piggledy way his legs are, laughs with awkward embarrassment, hears the grey-haired girl's friend mention something about the armchair again and passes out.

Chapter Twenty-Three

"Oh, is he dead?" Suki asks.
Georgina looks at her incredulously as she puts her phone away. "We'd still have to phone the emergency services, Suki Ambrosia Matsugane."
Suki reacts, the words like a slap. "How dare you use my full name?"
"Now is not the time for fuckery."
Suki puts on her best normal head and telephones the relevant people, Georgina runs through the events.
They were walking along chatting the only kind of shit that two friends who have known each other all their lives can talk about. Two friends who know of no one else evolved enough to even begin to understand and share their particular brand of unique absurdity, when the gargantuan circus lorry with the Freddy KRUEGER tent on it drove past them. Then, just as it was about to turn back onto the main road shit fell out from beneath it. Their initial reaction was that a part of the lorry's undercarriage had fallen off. Suki laughed for a full twenty seconds, especially when Georgina had used the word undercarriage. They ran on to take a look and when they got closer they saw the mess wasn't part of a lorry. A jumble of furniture parts, wheels and a man. Their second thought was it was a hit and run, bizarrely involving an armchair.
A six foot jam of blood spread across the tarmac and at either end were a man and his legs from the knees down.

MATTHEW CASH

He was elderly and had a big cowboy moustache and was somehow conscious for a moment.

"Ambulance is coming."
"Good," Georgina searches for something to put against the man's leg stumps but strangely enough they've already stopped bleeding. "Suki, give him your hoodie so he's warm."
"Fuck, no!" Suki says clutching hold of the turquoise garment she was wrapped in, she even pulls its hood up for further defiance. Two pink antennae flop down over her fringe. "This is a genuine Fooklebob hoodie from motherfucking Japan, George, they don't even make them anymore. I don't want old man blood and shit on it. Where was that thing from?"
Georgina sighs and unzips her coat and drapes it over the comatose pensioner. "Primarni."
"See. Always knew your cheapskate ways would help save a life."
"Shut the fuck up," Georgina grumbles, she like her cheapskate ways, "and for your information Fooklebob is far less superior than Joogoggami."
Suki recoils, hand on chest like she's taken an arrow. "Bitch."
They wait in silence for a few minutes and the man on the road begins to mutter a woman's name and then he scares the shit out of both of them by sitting bolt upright and roaring, "Greenfield you bastard."

FRANKIE SAYS DIE

Chapter Twenty-Four

He's out of his body with a jolt, he sees himself jogging over the small road towards the house. He's lighter than a summer breeze. He bobs several feet off the ground, wonders why he doesn't just blow away and then he sees a neon blue beam trailing like a ribbon, it sprouts from the centre of his chest and into the back of his earthly body. He is pulled along like a kite.

Tommy sees himself look down at the comatose dachshund. Floating above Zoltan's body is a facsimile, the original occupant of the dog's body, he runs around in circles in mid-air, a puppy again, yapping happily, free of pain at last.
The woman notices Zoltan on the driveway and yelps. "Oh my God, what's up with him?" She crouches and reaches out to the dog. Tommy wonders why the little dog flapping around above her head doesn't just follow the blue lead back down into his body.
Frankie knows he can't talk as Tommy so he mimes shivering and wraps his arms around himself. He lifts his t-shirt up and the woman grimaces as she sees Tommy's battered and bruised body.
"Bring him in the house," the lady says and the expression on her face screams pity.
"No," Tommy shrieks out a warning but no one can hear him. He's yanked behind his body as Frankie stoops to pick Zoltan up in his arms like a baby and quickly follows the woman into the house.

MATTHEW CASH

Tommy glides into a kitchen where two teenage girls suddenly gawp at the scruffy man carrying the dog.

"Oh my God, mum," one of them says, "you didn't hit it did you?"

"No," the woman snaps and runs over to a pile of folded laundry in the corner. She pulls out a thick blanket and lays it on the table. "Come on, let's get him wrapped up, poor thing."

Frankie nervously lowers Zoltan's body onto the table. Above and behind him Tommy shouts and waves his arms around to no avail, it's pointless but he can't help but try and warn them.

The woman takes over wrapping the still-breathing dachshund in the blanket whilst the two teenagers look on awkwardly. If Tommy had breath he would hold it in anticipation of what Frankie was going to do.

Frankie makes his move.

Whilst the three women are concentrating on the unconscious dog he silently steps to the cooker where the preparations for a meal are in process, he grabs the handle of a bubbling saucepan and flings the contents into one of the teenager's faces. Scalding water and potatoes cover her head and shoulders and the scream she makes is horrendous. Before anyone knows what's going on Frankie has pulled a knife from a block standing on a work surface and has thrust it up below the chin of the other girl. The older woman spins around, sees one girl's face erupting into a red mass of blisters and the other staggering around making a hissing whine through clenched teeth and a mouth that starts spurting copious amounts of blood. Tommy is a useless spectator, hovering near the dusty strip lighting as Frankie picks up a glass cutting board and smashes the older woman in the face with it. She falls

FRANKIE SAYS DIE

across the corner of the kitchen table and onto the floor but she's on her hands and knees immediately.
Tommy wants her to fight back, to hell with his fucking body.
She does. She grabs a chair and holds it out in front of her like a lion tamer. The two girls still spin around her in pained hysteria, she positions herself between them and Frankie who is scanning the room for something else to use as a weapon. He yanks open a cutlery drawer but the woman thrusts with the chair causing the contents to spill on the tiles. Frankie grins and Tommy feels himself instantly sucked back into his body.
The woman jabs with the chair, the leg slides into Tommy's screaming mouth, he flaps his hands about to try and get purchase on the piece of furniture, to tell her it's okay now, he's in charge of his body, but the woman is a enraged, she shoves him backwards against the wall. The chair leg clogs the back of his throat and vomit explodes around it. He manages to grab the thing and tear it away from her and she's suddenly on the floor screaming. Tommy thinks he hurt her when he pulled the chair away but she's grabbing the backs of her legs. Both of her achilles tendons have been sliced through. Frankie's back in Zoltan now and the little dog runs in circles around the kitchen, tail swishing, with a serrated knife in his mouth. Tommy rushes to stop the dog but on his latest ring around the table, now he's brought the woman down to his level, he's slit her throat. Tommy stares hopelessly at the woman choking on her own blood and the two shrieking girls. With a jolt Tommy's back on the fucking ceiling watching Frankie use his body to calmly rifle through the fallen cutlery and pick

up the the biggest knives. He pushes the girl with the melting face onto the table and plants the foot long blade into her chest. Tommy hears it enter the wood beneath her. The last girl is slumped against a freezer which has a separate fridge stacked on top. Frankie grabs her by the hair, opens the fridge door and repeatedly slams it on her head. Aside from knocking someone who's already white with blood loss and shock about it doesn't really do anything so he lays her on the floor and pushes the fridge off the freezer onto her. Her head explodes with a crunch like a piñata.

Tommy's frozen on the ceiling, looking down at the scene of carnage that took such a small amount of time to create. Frankie's beneath him arms stretched wide, drinking in whatever his kind reap from murder. Zoltan's husk lies discarded in the corner, a stuffed toy with a muzzle covered in blood, his little ghost hovers above him cowering.

Tommy hears a noise like a boiled egg being sucked through a hosepipe and he's back behind his eyes in the centre seat to the massacre around him, Zoltan stretches and gets to his feet.

How's that? Frankie says cheerfully in Tommy's head.
Tommy can't answer, he's numb.

The front door opens and a fat man carrying a baby in a car seat takes three steps into the house before stopping and seeing the strange, scruffy man with blood on him in his house. They stare at one another for what feels like a century. Frankie woofs and distracts the man in time to jump back into Tommy's body and sprint up the hallway. The man's immediate reaction is to step aside from the open door and shield his baby from the unknown assailant but this intruder isn't ready to leave.

FRANKIE SAYS DIE

Frankie slams the door shut and pushes the man into the house, he falls onto the stairs.

Tommy can see this man isn't a fighter, tears are already rolling as he cowers but still he tries to protect the baby with his sizable bulk.

Frankie picks up a big china vase that sits on the sill of a small window and lifts it above the man's head. The man strikes out with a foot and kicks Frankie square in the balls, it's unexpected, the vase smashes at his feet.

"Get out of my house," the man shouts standing up and pointing towards the door as menacing as he can.

Tommy knows he should have carried on with the attack. Frankie straightens up, two jagged shards from the vase in his hand, and slices them criss-cross across the man's fat neck.

His fingers grope the deep laceration feebly for a second before blood starts decorating his hallway.

Frankie throws him aside, picks the baby carrier up off the stairs and walks back into the kitchen dragging Tommy in the air behind him.

Without a second thought Frankie switches the oven on and opens the door. He takes the chubby little baby boy out of the carrier, yanks the metal racks from the oven interior, puts him inside, and shuts the door.

MATTHEW CASH

FRANKIE SAYS DIE

Chapter Twenty-Five

Ray Greenfield steps onto the grass to survey the land that will be his for the next two weeks. His leather trousers creak as he crouches and lays a palm against the ground. It's been dry for a few weeks which is good, there will be no problems setting up. His entourage will be with him shortly, they always travel ten minutes behind their ringmaster.
"Looks like the weather will be fair, Ray."
Ray smiles at his wife. "Fair for the fayre."
Rochelle Greenfield takes his hand, she is a raven-haired beauty with hints of Lily Munster and Morticia Addams about her. "Where will my tent go?"
"Wherever you like it, my dear."
Rochelle points towards a giant oak towering over the field. "Beneath that tree."
"As you wish."
She looks with trepidation as the first of the circus convoy enters the park. "Do you think we'll get him to come back?"
Ray squeezes her hand. "Of course. As soon as they're here I'm going to send the clowns out to scout and tout."
"Won't he recognise them?"
"No, they weren't part of the trope when Tommy rode with us."
"You said Boinky has always been with you, been here for generations, you said. Surely he'll recognise him."
"Ah, no, not Boinky. Boinky is a true clown, the father of all clowns, that's true but even Boinky has learnt the uses of makeup and magic to manipulate and disguise."

Rochelle puts her arms around her husband and runs her fingers along his white streak. Ray curls a hand around her hip.

A Volkswagen camper van painted in jagged rainbow stripes bumps over the potholes in the park entrance, weaves manically between the slow-moving lorries and its driver honks its novelty hooter. A red speaker on the roof sounds a comedy BOING.

"Here they come," Rochelle says with childlike excitement. "Here come the clowns."

FRANKIE SAYS DIE

Chapter Twenty-Six

The circus has changed a lot over the years, especially since Ray took over from his dad and it makes Boinky sad. Being an eternal provider of entertainment has its toll. All his friends have come and gone, even the special ones who were with him from the very start of his conjuring. Albatross Steve and Gormless Pete, Glad Harry, Mr Rapey, Farmer Spacklecock they were all gone but Boinky just keeps going on and on with a permanent grin on his face. Which is ironic as he's really, really angry

He feels like a cult member who has spent decades under the brainwashing influence of some psychotic David Koresh wannabe. When he had been just a few minutes old that evil sadist Francis Foster had seen him for what he was and filled his vacant, but absorbent, mind with the most grotesque of imagery and ideas. The Old Acts were created and shaped with those ideals in mind and in turn their souls recycled into his clowns.

But over the centuries Boinky has learnt better.

He isn't as free to be himself these days, he wears patchwork rainbow dungarees, still wears his tutu for special occasions but understands that times have changed. His children are dependent on him. Ray says so. But Boinky can't help but see the bright side of things, he has a whole new family of friends now, Mr Crackers is back at home in the aviary with his wife and kids.

Everybody else is happy.

MATTHEW CASH

It's not so bad though, he really loves his van, Persephone. It's the first girlfriend he's ever had. Captain Flimbo is still as raunchy as ever though, always helping out in times of need, whispering helpful hints to make his act even better. Boinky looks in the rear view mirror at his children. His squadron of clowns has grown since Ray took over. There's four in total and each one fills him with tearful, paternal pride. They're different to the Old Acts, each one contains a part of him. His two smiles curve upwards as he remembers liberating each of them from their birth parents.

Libby had been a squirmy wormy in her buggy outside a bakery in a town he can't remember but he does remember the magic trick he performed which swapped her with a marrow and still convinced her parents they were pushing their child around. He often laughs thinking just how long her parents would have carried on living their lives with their marrow-child, the whole world thinking they were insane. After a few months when their baby fell apart would they have had a little marrow funeral?

"Now look at 'er," Captain Flimbo chuckles heartily, "ain't no baby now and them knockers are more like pumpkins than marrows."

Boinky would rather Captain Flimbo not talk about his daughter's breasts that way. Boinky had learnt a lot recently, especially since learning to read, that was called being a sexist perverted cunt.

Libby was beautiful, his pride and joy, with her pink afro that was so big it billowed across the interior of the van like a candyfloss cloud.

FRANKIE SAYS DIE

Box hunches beneath her wayward hair. Boinky had used the same swapping trick when freeing him from his birth parents but that time he used a dead pigeon.
Box was huge, even bigger than Glad Harry had been in his prime and that was big. He was the clown strongman and there was nothing particularly funny about his appearance generally aside from the fact that he had the upper torso of the Incredible Hulk and the legs of a five year old.

Moopy he swapped with someone else's baby which he had previously swapped with a bag that he pulled out of a magical red bin with a picture of doggos on it. Moopy was big and chubby and cute, he always dresses up like a baby because he looks like a baby aside from his one central eye. The cyclops thing was an effect from the ancient clownic initiation ritual, each one of Boinky's clowns had something special to show for that.

Mr Fumble is a naughty one, a cheeky little monster, with hands everywhere. He was always grabbing people and poking them in naughty places and never getting caught due to his six invisible arms. When behaving himself people would marvel at his magical juggling skills and how he seemed to be able to make objects fly around him with the power of his mind.

They each had their ways and clowned properly when the need was there and Boinky loved them all equally.
He teases a fingertip over Persephone's buttons and dials, she likes that, and gently presses the horn. The BOING

makes his whole family laugh. Boinky feels Persephone rub against his crotch as the van bounces over the uneven ground and feels himself BOING too. Today's a hap-hap-happy day.

Chapter Twenty-Seven

The little baby kicks against the inside of the oven door a few times before settling down and just staring at the dim orange bulb above it. Tommy's fingers twiddle the temperature up to maximum and Frankie lets him back into his body.

Without any hesitation Tommy switches the oven off but before he has a chance to open the door Zoltan waddles over to nose it back closed.

Don't even think about taking it out of the oven. Frankie stares through the dachshund's eyes. *That's what you call my insurance.*

Tommy hurts all over from the physical exertion his body has been put through but most of all his balls are killing him from where the man kicked him. "Please, don't hurt the baby."

Well you know what you have to do, don't you? If you don't agree to say my words then the baby gets roasted.

Tommy has no choice, he is powerless compared to Frankie. "Can't it be anyone other than Georgina?"

Tell you what, I'll let you poke her once I'm inside her body.

"That's… No."

It's the only reason you don't want me to possess her.

"She's my friend."

Tough.

"And if I don't you'll continue doing stuff like this. With my body?"

Mate, today was all improvisation, Frankie shakes his head and sets those great big ears flapping. *Imagine what I can do with a little consideration. All this was nothing in the grand scheme of things. I've produced fucking artwork before. I've got it all under my belt, and have had five centuries to hone my skills. I've done stuff that'd make Ed Gein blush.*

"Okay, I'll do it." Tommy sighs.

Right, come on chap. There's a working phone box at the end of the road where you can phone this in. Frankie readies to leave the house, *That's if you want to get someone to save the baby. I mean I don't know how long it'll survive shutting the oven like that, even without the heating turned on.*

"Okay, okay," Tommy follows the dog out of the house trying to guess what to do next. There's got to be a way to stop this. There has to be.

There isn't, Frankie reads his mind. *And enough of that sort of thinking or I'll jump back into you and bake the brat.*

"Sorry."

Right, Frankie moves away from the house, *let's start practising. These words may sound like complete bollocks to someone as degenerate as you but, trust me, they're not. And pronunciation is integral to the mantra. You say it wrong it don't fucking work. So, the first word is a piece of piss. Cashtella. Think of bank tellers...*

"Cashtella," Tommy repeats half-heartedly.

A little more emphasis on the last syllable please, Frankie says, sounding like a school teacher. *We need to find somewhere we can hold up whilst you practice.*

Tommy suggests an old shop he sometimes squats in, they'll be alone and uninterrupted.

At the furthest reaches of his mind, somewhere he hopes Frankie can't reach, he hopes he'll think of a way to thwart the maniac.

FRANKIE SAYS DIE

Chapter Twenty-Eight

Norman is livid. After spending however many hours under anaesthetic the doctors tell him he's also broken his hip as well as knackered both of his legs. Twenty fucking years of this now, no matter what. Greenfield knew exactly what he was doing when he gave him the witch doctor's elixir.

The only shining light is Gloria who has been by his bedside since the accident. Accident. That's what he's had to say it was despite the two girls contradicting his claims and mentioning the bloody armchair. Just an accident. Gloria clutches his hand and his eyes light on her ring finger. Tommy said to act quick.

"Marry me, Gloria," Norman implores.

For a second she looks grave, like he's about to die, maybe that's what she's thinking, maybe that's what makes her say yes. No, Tommy said it was the real thing. Norman smiles through the oxygen mask. All this is a small price to pay for twenty years of happiness with this beauty.

FRANKIE SAYS DIE

Chapter Twenty-Nine

Georgina takes the bundle of flyers out of the cellophane bag. Each one has a photo and information about Zoltan. There's nothing else she can do now but hope he turns up. The police have no idea who killed her mum and her dad was still with them helping them with their enquiries. Suki has taken the day off work to help continue the search for Georgina's dog and when she greets her friend on the High Street she has a secretive look about her like she's hiding something.

"What's up with you?" Georgina asks her and hands her some flyers.

"Been reading about serial killers."

"Oh, the usual thing that makes a Suki tick then?"

"Yep. Wanna know something weird?"

"I already know something weird, you."

"You're hilari-arse." Suki tuts. "It's about The Smiler."

"Go on, tell me something about my favourite serial killer."

"Well, as you know, he had been doing his thing since the late seventies but get this, just before The Smiler murders began they found the mutilated body of a copper in the back of his patrol car."

"He started out by nailing a pig, so what? You're not going to tell me you think his reign of terror is all one big anti-establishment bollocks, are you?"

"No, no. The policeman was found with his liver missing."

Georgina frowns, not sure she gets the point Suki is trying to make but then it sinks in. "The same as The Smiler tried to make me eat his?"
"Exactly."
"Okay, well obviously the guy was fucked up, you know, killing people isn't exactly normal, and he was, like, one hundred years old so maybe he had some form of dementia which made him try and kill me, his last victim, in a special way to close the circle. Maybe the liver had some meaning to him."
Suki screws her face up in disgust."That sounds entirely rational. I don't like it."
"So, what's your theory?"
"Well, I kept reading about weird, brutal deaths and murderers, as I do, and found another one in a town near to where the policeman was found in the early fifties. Another man with parts of his liver ripped out and get this. They found remnants with teeth marks in them. And they weren't the deceased's."
"So, what do you think, this is some cult or something?"
Suki shrugs, "I've no idea, it's only been like twenty four hours and I can only go by what I can find online."
"Okay, well keep checking whilst we stick these flyers around, you've got me intrigued now. We could be like Daphne and Velma—"
"I'm Velma," Suki interrupts, "I've got the dark hair and glasses.
Georgina groans, she's not going to get into this argument with Suki again. Something they'd fought about since kids, they both wanted to be the nerdy one.
"Okay, I'll be Shaggy. Let's go rescue Scooby and uncover this secret cult of liver-eating feathermuckers."

Chapter Thirty

Boinky stands to attention like a royal guard, chin up, eyes wide, arms straight at his sides, his children try to do the same but they aren't as disciplined as him.
Ray Greenfield's their drill sergeant, he walks along the line of clowns twice before addressing Boinky.
"Your family are looking fit and healthy, Boinky," he says, stopping in front of the stocky clown. Boinky nods with feverish excitement and a muffled grumble comes from the belly of his dungarees.
It's the first time Rochelle has been introduced to Boinky and his troop and she frowns at her husband. Ray smiles and checks that they are secluded by the ring of circus lorries. "Go on, Boinky, let the Captain out so we can hear him."
Boinky chuckles and pulls the top of his dungarees down to expose his giant belly and the face of Captain Flimbo. "Alright, Ray, long time no see."
Boinky's belly ripples and wobbles in time with the gruff voice that seems to come from his navel.
The tattooed clown-face is like nothing Rochelle has ever seen. Two faded blue cartoon eyes cover Boinky's breasts, his nipples inked a darker blue for his pupils, a nose that was once red is now a fist-sized, swollen green, weeping sore, his navel just off to one side leaking a thick yellow pus. Captain Flimbo's mouth was a vast, black-lipped expanse complete with a lime green salivating tongue and piratical teeth. It spread over the bottom of the flab

overhanging Boinky's abdomen and up to where his ribs should be.

"It's like ventriloquism," Ray whispers in Rochelle's ear. "Boinky himself has never uttered a word. Captain Flimbo is the one who does all the talking."

"That's extraordinary, you think it's like a multiple personality thing?"

"We can never know. Like I say, Boinky is a mystery, there's not a lot to be known about him and his kind other than what us puny humans have tried to mimic. And got wrong." Ray turns back to Boinky who stares into the distance drooling now Captain Flimbo was in control.

"Right then, boss, what's the plan for these bunch of cunts?"

"You can see him wobbling his belly with his hands," Rochelle whispers.

Ray looks at her coldly.

"I'll go and supervise the erection of the tent." Rochelle gathers her skirts and storms off.

"She can supervise my erection," Captain Flimbo snorts.

"That's my wife, Captain."

"Terribly sorry, Ray, you know I can never control this gob o' mine."

"You are forgiven, old friend. You and Boinky's brood are to go to town, flaunt your talents and tricks as usual when we set up somewhere new but whilst you are doing so, I want you to look out for Tommy."

Boinky snaps to attention at the sound of the name.

"Tommy, eh? You've finally found him," Captain Flimbo sounds serious for once.

"Indeed I have."

"You gonna, you know?" Captain Flimbo makes a weird little noise whilst Boinky slides his thumb across his throat.

FRANKIE SAYS DIE

This time Ray looks Boinky in the eyes, can see the evident sadness there, fear even. "No, Boinky, no. He's like a son to me and I know he's very special to you. I want him to come back to us. Back to his family."
Boinky smiles and tears ooze from the corners of his eyes.
"Oh god, ignore that sentimental bastard," Captain Flimbo groans. "Daft prick. I'll make sure he rallies the gang together. We're going incognito, I take it?"
Ray looks at the momentarily silent band of mutated clown-flesh, knowing full well that just one glimpse of them in their natural state would send the public into complete lunacy. "Yes, that's for the best."

Chapter Thirty-Two

"*Cashtella mogga blixa f'loggon,*" Tommy repeats the first sentence of Frankie's ritual. "What the fuck do these words actually mean? What language is it?"

If I told you that I'd have to kill you, Frankie offers light-heartedly.

"Aren't you going to do that anyway?" Tommy has seen what the warlock is capable of, knows he'll be disposed of as soon as he's not useful.

I never said that. Did I say that? The little dog looks up at him with stupid, canine innocence.

"I just assumed."

Well don't, Frankie pauses, *although, chances are, you'll be the first to get it once I've taken over the girl, but don't worry the offer still stands.*

"What offer?"

Poking her.

Tommy turns away in disgust. "I don't want to—"

Yes you do, I can read your mind. You think about living with her and everything.

"Yeah, Georgina, her. Her personality. Not with you inside her. It's not just a physical thing."

Ah well, if you change your mind I promise to keep my word just as long as you ain't got the clap or any of those dodgy tramp diseases.

"I haven't."

Good.

Tommy can't help but think Frankie is distracting him from his original question. "You don't know anything about these magic words of yours, do you?"

Of course I— no. Look, I don't give a flying fuck if they're Martian or Lithuanian, mate, they fucking work, I've used them loads of times successfully.

"Aren't you interested? They could mean something really silly."

Mate, I don't care if they're Satan's shopping list. They work. It's all that matters.

"What if it's not the words that are magic but you?"

Course I'm magic, so are the words though.

"Yeah, but when you're saying them I bet you're thinking about what they are supposed to do."

Well, duh, I'm usually elbow-deep in my own guts when I'm saying them so it'd be hard not to.

"So what if I just think about something entirely random when saying them?"

Frankie stops and makes growls at him. *Well you'd better fucking well think about soul-swapping and the consumption of livers, hadn't you?*

Tommy smiles. Because if I don't you will end up mutilating yourself and bleeding to death.

You're a dickhead, aren't you? I'm not going to be mutilating nothing, you are. You're going to be chanting this shit whilst force-feeding the girl her dog's liver.

"Bollocks."

Chapter Thirty-Three

The high street is busier than usual, a crowd is congregating around a podium where a piece of modern art was installed twenty years previous, now it's just a gathering place for litter and degenerates. Tommy carries past the onlookers, he has no interest in whatever band or performance is capturing their attention but a splash of green hair catches his eye.
"Oh God, no," he says quickening his pace, "not fucking clowns." He steers away from the show, ignores the excited noise of the crowd, he doesn't want anything to do with clowns. He checks that Zoltan is following him and walks smack bang into one doing tricks amidst the people. Tommy really can't understand how he missed it. The clown's female and what a female she is. She towers over him and looks as though she must be at least a size thirty. She wears a red dress with white stars on it and is making balloon animals for the people surrounding her at an unnatural speed, Tommy has never seen anyone move so quick. Her hair is puffed up behind her in two pink buns that make him think of mickey mouse ears. For a moment he's mesmerised by the blur of her hands and the speed in which she blows the balloons up, it's almost like she's regurgitating them rather than raising the limp vessels to her big painted lips. Everyone around him is so happy, the smiles on their faces are so wide that he can't see their eyes.

Cheering pulls Tommy's attention from the balloon clown and he stares at the another on the podium who is doing something impossible.

Tommy knows the world record for juggling balls is eleven at once but the green-haired clown is doing a lot more than that. He pushes his way through the people barely registering Zoltan's barking. The clown has too many things in the air, there are balls, apples, eggs, beanbags and they are moving too fast.

"It's impossible."

Frankie is yapping, at his heels, a dog possessed.

Tommy knows there's something off about these entertainers.

Behind the superhuman juggler a clown the size of a gorilla picks up a passing black cab and holds it above his head, the driver looks equally stunned and impressed from the cab's window.

Tommy grabs the dachshund by his collar and turns to leave. "I've got a funny feeling about this, we need to-"

A huge gut in patchwork dungarees blocks his path. The man's face is crudely covered in thick pink paint, several shades darker than the skin on his exposed arms and shoulders. It takes him by surprise but he recognises the shape of the man's features beneath the makeup.

"Boinky," he whispers before an almighty racket distracts him once again. He turns, just for a second to see another clown wearing nothing but a nappy wailing amidst the horde of happy, laughing people. Thick blubbery arms wrap around him from behind and he hears a voice, muffled like it's talking through a mask or cloth. He hasn't heard it in years.

"Come on Tommy, time to come home."

FRANKIE SAYS DIE

The audience are literally rolling on the concrete, an over-exaggerated parody of what laughter should be, tears cover their cheeks, piss soaks through clothing but they clutch their balloon animals and laugh, laugh, laugh. Laugh at the clowns, because they are fucking funny, laugh at the adult baby, the impossible juggler, the strongman as he hurls the black cab into the front of a slowing bus, laugh at the little sausage dog who runs circles around the big guy carrying the skinny man like a naughty child.
They laugh themselves silly.

FRANKIE SAYS DIE

Chapter Thirty-Four

Frankie smelt it the second Tommy joined the crowd. Magic has its own unique smell that can't be described by mere words. The closest you can get to putting in a way the normal person would understand is this analogy; take the smell of walking through a forest on the coldest winter day and combine it with slamming your face into a brick wall as hard as you can until you knock yourself out. Whilst eating Liquorice Allsorts.
If there was a way of concocting a scenario in which there was a brick wall in the middle of a forest in which to smack your face against then the smell, just before you pass out, with a gob crammed full of aniseed mash, would be the closest you could get to the smell of magic.
To the untrained nose obviously.
Frankie learned the smell back in his warlock days, there was a lot more raw, real magic around those days and certain people reeked of it. But he hasn't smelt it in centuries, and discovering that scent, made even stronger through his canine senses, temporarily stuns him.
Another magician, whether it be witch, warlock or something else could mean trouble, his kind rarely works with others despite the old ideals of covens and satanic cults.
But it could also mean help.
He follows his nose, not really knowing what to expect; an old wizard or maybe one of these new age healers who had

perhaps accidentally tapped into something archaic whilst mixing ingredients from Holland and Barratt.
He never suspected the fucking clowns until all the townfolk started acting weird, literally falling to the ground in convulsions, but then the strong one threw a taxi through the front of a bus window and the next thing he knew Tommy was being carried off in a fireman's lift. And what made things a thousand times worse was he recognised the thing's swagger.
He conjured the fucking thing half a millennium ago.

He gives chase, tries his best to swap into Tommy and hopefully use some of his skills in physical combat to free himself from his captors but the fear of Zoltan's body getting trampled amongst the delusional crowd, or getting beyond the reach of his projection skills prevents that. He sees the thing bundle Tommy into a rainbow VW camper and speed away.
There 2 nothing he can do, so he does the natural thing any dog would do.
He heads home.

The problem is Frankie doesn't know where home is. Sure he was there with Georgina the day before but that doesn't mean he remembers where it is.
He knows Zoltan will be floating around his body somewhere. He learnt the misery of the afterlife years before from the only genuine spiritual medium he's ever known. It is one of the reasons he refuses to die and sought a loophole.
Spirits, souls, essences, or whatever they really are, of anything that's alive can not move on to the next realm until their earthly remains are gone in their entirety. The

FRANKIE SAYS DIE

amount of ancient ghosts that are still bound to their buried remains is phenomenal. The spectral crowds above graveyards are horrendous.
Only way to free yourself from yourself was cremation or something equally as destructive.
Maybe, if he relaxed his will a bit, Zoltan could slip back in and help him out.
At this point anything was worth a try.
He takes shelter in a doorway and lets down the few mental defences he's put up since commandeering the dachshund. He can feel Zoltan close-by but senses that the dog is nervous.
It's okay, Zee. Let's go find Georgina.
He imagines the dog's head cocking to one side when Georgina is mentioned and Zoltan's thoughts mingle with Frankie's own. He sees Georgina through the little dog's eyes. Hears her talk a distortion of words that make no sense aside from one or two that he has been trained to understand.
Food.
Treat.
Good boy.
Zee.
BAD DOG.
And thankfully, *Home.*
Let's go home, Zee. Good boy. Frankie can almost feel the dog bouncing with anticipation.

MATTHEW CASH

Chapter Thirty-Five

Norman feels his heart sink as Gloria offers him her engagement ring on a shaking palm. The tears come before the words, they've always been easier to produce at times like these.
"I'm sorry, love," Gloria says, her face a slack grey mask.
He doesn't take the ring. "What's happened? I thought we were good."
She looks at him with the most sorrowful of eyes. "Oh, we were. You are everything to me, my old rocker."
"So what's this about? Is it my legs, cuz that's not going to stop me from getting about. I've got that mobility scooter in the garage."
"It's not you. I love you, I love listening to all your daft tales about biker gangs and what not." Gloria closes her fingers around the engagement ring. "I came here for the test results for what I thought was IBS."
"Oh God," his words are barely audible.
Gloria nods. "Cancer. They reckon about six months tops. I'm not having chemo, Norman, I can't. I remember what it did to my mum."
Norman feels like he's going to explode. He's angry, he's brokenhearted.
Tommy said it was the real thing.
But he also said not to hang about.
"You get that bloody ring back on that finger Gloria and get the first fucking date they can get us in at the registry office."

MATTHEW CASH

"What?" she laughs.

"You heard me." He reaches forward, clasps her hands in his, and slips the ring back on her finger. "I'm going to give you the best six months of your life."

Gloria collapses into him and he holds her in his arms, arms that are covered in ancient daggers, skulls and snakes. Tattoos that look ridiculous on such an old frail man but the irony of it all is he doesn't feel old and frail, he feels like he did forty years ago, full of rage and fury, anger at everyone and everything, anger at the injustice in the world.

This is Ray Greenfield's doing, he knows that full well. He's stupid to expect anything else from the twisted ringmaster, almost every reward he has given him over the years has come with dire consequences.

But this time the circus leader won't get away with it, for Norman has drunk his special elixir and is nigh on invincible for the next twenty years and he's determined to have that silver-toothed twat's head if it's the last thing he does.

He ignores the protests from the people at the hospital and discharges himself. They've done all the work they need to do, pins, staples, stitches, it's enough. It's not like he's going to die of blood loss or anything. His mind is a fever-dream of plans, too many things come all at once but he allows them and acknowledges them regardless. What's paramount is that he and Gloria get wedded and that he uses the money he's sat on for so long to make sure she lives in comfort for what little time she has left.

Once those bowls are hurtling along somehow he'll get himself into his garage, throw himself on the floor if he has to, and see about dusting off his tools and mechanical skills.

MATTHEW CASH

Chapter Thirty-Six

"The police think that maybe The Smiler had an accomplice."
Georgina is horrified by what her dad's just said. "And that's who killed mum?"
Her dad nods. "They're keeping the house under surveillance and want you to make sure you're extra vigilant when going out and about."
"I can't believe this." Maybe there really is something in this Liver Cult Suki was delving into. "I need to go out and find—"
They both hear the barking from the front door.
"—Zee?" Georgina rushes across the house and tears the door open.
Zoltan sits on the doormat looking like the goodest boy ever. They take in each other for a single second before the dog launches itself at her, peddling at her knees with his front paws, yapping excitedly and pissing all over her shoes.

"Oh, my god," her dad says, crouching down to fuss him. "He's filthy and, shit, is that blood?"
Georgina inspects the grime that covers the dog's short coat, sure enough it looks like spots of dry blood. She immediately checks for any wounds but is thankful not to find any. "I don't think it's his." She picks him up and cradles him against her chest, "Oh my baby, I've missed

you so much. Did you chase Mummy's killer? You're a good boy, a very good boy."

"Don't wash him," her dad says racing for the phone. "He might have evidence on him. If he did go after the guy that killed your mum then his DNA might still be on him."

"Good thinking, Dad."

Suki is happy that Georgina's got her little liver-eating hobo back but she's too engrossed in her latest research to dwell on it too much.

Little things are being unearthed now she is focusing on the consumption of human livers.

Ancient rituals, dating back to the Mesopotamian times, speak of how eating certain parts of your enemies are supposed to both spiritually and physically benefit you. They believed that you could gain your enemy's power and knowledge by eating specific parts like their heart and brains. Some tribes ate their dead as a form of respect and a way to remember the person they once were, to keep a part of them within them.

There aren't a lot of references to liver eating in particular but the ones that do crop up are frightening and vaguely similar but it is England's most notorious serial killer that gives her a glimpse of something bigger.

Mary Kelly, Jack the Ripper's last supposed victim was found mutilated with her organs all strewn around her but her heart was never found. Suki's searching discovers a theory that it was actually her liver that was never found, not her heart. This internet wormhole leads her to talk of rituals involving soul transference and how eating another person's innards whilst performing a particular act of black magic can enable that person to take over a new host. It

FRANKIE SAYS DIE

makes no sense at all. Why would you want to eat someone's liver so they could possess you? But then she turns it on the flipside. If you made someone eat your liver, like, say you were an old man and fed it to a baby, you could live your life all over again.
There seriously can't be people around today who believe this shit?
If there really is a cult that thought they could pass themselves on by making someone else eat their livers then surely they wouldn't be around for much longer?
But why kill Georgina's mum? Cuz she got in the way when they came to get Georgina?
It's madness, absolute madness.
Suki laughs at her computer screen, and remembers Georgina telling her about The Smiler's crazy chanting.
He believed in this shit.
And Zee ate his fucking liver.

MATTHEW CASH

Chapter Thirty-Seven

He's shoved in the back of the van and the clowns bundle in behind him. None of them are normal, they've all been Boinkerized.

The female balloonist claps her hands together at the speed of an autistic stim, laughs as she unfastens something behind her head and her pink hair erupts across the interior. It obscures her eyes but not her ecstatic grin.

The clown wearing nothing but a nappy flops down beside her and Tommy finds it impossible not to stare at his single eye. A thick yellow crust circles the large orb, clusters of it cling to eyelashes so long they poke out over his nose. He laughs, a childish baby squeal, his mouth a shapeless hole with one single tooth the size of a fingertip, and fumbles at the lady clown's dress.

Without any hesitation she whips it up exposing herself. Huge, pale-white flesh running with blue varicose veins and a minge that runs from navel to mid-thigh.

The adult baby heaves up a tit the size of a potato sack and clamps his mouth around the already lactating nipple. Tommy recoils and the nursing clown guffaws and squeezes her other festering teet and squirts rank yellow milk in his face. Tommy gags on a mouthful of something that tastes like off-cheese and sweat and turns in time to see the juggler pounce on him.

The juggler is the most normal-looking of Boinky's brood, he's in proportion, unlike the rest of the bunch for one, his hair is spiky and green and the only clown makeup he

wears is his red painted nose, but he's managing to pin Tommy down without using his hands, so it seems.
Tommy can feel hands all over him though, they grab his arms and legs and there are even some left over to grab his testicles. He may appear normal for one of Boinky's lot but when Tommy looks into his eyes he can see the insanity trying to leap out like a jack-in-the-box.
Tommy strains towards the front of the van where Boinky drives, the strongman clown fills up the majority of the cabin. "Boinky, what the hell did you do?"
"Make him go sleep, make him go sleep," the baby clown shouts after a loud pop of the female clown's tit leaving his mouth.
The juggler giggles and Tommy feels one of his invisible, ghost hands release him and hears the tearing of material. His laughter reaches a crescendo when he dangles a large pair of ripped yellow y-fronts in Tommy's face. They're covered in a rorschach scribble of multi-coloured skidmarks. The juggler thrusts the material over Tommy's mouth and nose and the smell is intoxicating, nauseating anaesthetising.
Within seconds he feels his consciousness float away like a big old bunch of balloons.

Whilst he's out cold he relives his past, his escape and the massacre of Greenfield Circus. He sees them all, all the old gang, the Old Acts that came to the world along with Boinky, the special souls who found their way to the circus like Albatross Steve and Glad Harry. He remembers them. Remembers the end of it all.

FRANKIE SAYS DIE

"Please, Ray, I can't do another one. Something's wrong with my head," Tommy pleads as Ray grabs him by the nape of his neck.

"Last one of the day, Tomboy, then I'll give you something that will knock you out until that headache of yours is gone." Ray straightens Tommy up and brushes down his black suit.

Tommy doesn't want to do another reading. They've started making him feel ill for hours afterwards, worse than the hangover he gets from the booze Ray gives him to take the pain away.

Ray frogmarches him across muddy grass towards a small green and red striped tent. A poster near the entrance tells the world this is where The Boy Who Sees performs his readings.

"Now, don't let me down. That's Jeremy Clifton in there, piss him off he could destroy us."

"Please, Ray, I can't."

"Get in there!" Ray shoves him through the tent opening and Jeremy Clifton's two burly body guards jump to attention, their hands dart inside their jackets for the guns they carry.

"Sorry for the delay," Tommy chuckles nervously and moves across the small space.

Between the two guards sits a balding man in his sixties, wearing sunglasses. Jeremy Clifton is the town's crime lord, all around big-time gangster.

"Evening, boy," he says, reminding Tommy of the Tall Man from the Phantasm films.

Tommy takes his seat and tries his best to ignore the throbbing across his temples. He smiles at Clifton. "Are

there any aspects in particular you would like me to focus on? Wealth? Health? Love? Business?"
Clifton leans forwards and lays the back of his hand on the table. "Oh, let's have a bit of everything, shall we?"
"Er, I usually do readings from a personal item rather than a physical connection," Tommy begins awkwardly, reading people through touch has become unbearable of late, "A watch or piece of jewellery maybe?"
"I ain't taking my fucking watch off and there's nothing more personal than my fucking hand, son," Clifton snaps and grabs Tommy's own.
He's already in the mindset to read so as soon as the connection is made it's like shaking hands with a lightning bolt. He feels like he's being electrocuted, his body goes rigid but Clifton keeps hold of him tight, Tommy barely registers the heavies holding him down on the chair. His eyes roll backwards and he feels himself begin to convulse. The images come, lancing white hot arrows that penetrate his brain.
"Fire, so much fire and death. You're all going to die soon, very soon. The young ones are coming for you Clifton and they'll string you up like Jesus and light you up like the fucking Blackpool illuminations."
"Get him off me!"
Tommy hears the gang boss scream but he can't stop the torrent that comes from his mouth. "They'll get them all, Jeremy. Sally and the kids will be raped and tortured in front of you."
Rough hands try to separate him from Clifton. One of his fingers is snapped back and he doesn't feel a thing. "Oh my god, it takes so long for them to die. There's so much blood. Little Henry's the last to go, they use the iron Sally does your shirts with, they—" Tommy is thrown off and

FRANKIE SAYS DIE

away from the table. He begins to come round from his visions the moment the bond is broken, he sees Clifton and his men looming over him a second before they start putting the boots in.
The pain of their kicks is nothing compared to what's in his head.

Ray comes running into the tent to see what the commotion is all about and immediately starts grovelling at Clifton.
"He's ill, he's ill. I'm so sorry Jeremy, I should have said."
"You're going to pay for this Greenfield," Clifton shouts and leads his men from the tent.
Ray leaves Tommy to buck and bray on the grass but as he walks away Tommy's fingertips brush his ankle and for a second he sees the guns that will bring Ray Greenfield's circus down.

But they obviously didn't bring it down completely.

Tommy had been on the cusp of puberty when the visions, his readings, became painful. He had been their child prodigy, their star act. The Boy Who Sees. People paid good money for his readings. The rest of the circus did well but it was nothing out of the ordinary. A funfair took the majority of the cash and everyone had their own special roles to play. Boinky had always been Boinky though, but Boinky was a different Boinky when performing in the ring. He was a jolly, white faced clown with blue fuzzy hair who was an expert in ventriloquism and conjuring the silliest of objects out of audience members' pockets and behind their ears. They all had normal circus acts apart from the last night of their tour where the special acts were allowed to be themselves, let themselves go, recharge their unearthly powers for another year. Mystifico the magician reverted back to Mr Rapey, and Firenzo the lion tamer went back to Farmer Spacklecock. Steve the acrobat became the Albatross.

In that brief moment he had seen the end to that era of the circus, knew that however improbable and magical some of the performers were, they were no match for heavy calibre bullets. As soon as he was able to push himself up off the grass Tommy took off, ran away crying into the stormy night.

FRANKIE SAYS DIE

Chapter Thirty-Eight

It's not long before things start falling into an annoyingly twee routine. The police come and have a brief look at his dishevelled fur but don't do anything other than suggest Georgina give him a bath which results in him getting a smack on the nose for getting a boner when she is soaping him up.

Another problem surfaces when he lets Zoltan back in to use his homing skills. Frankie can't expel him. It's like now the little dog is back in his body he's clinging on to it with all four paws. It's like being a schizophrenic, or suffering with multiple personalities, except you're aware of your other persona - and it's a dog.

Georgina's dad has fallen into a deep depression following his wife's murder and spends most of his time lying on the sofa drinking strong coffee and watching day time television. Frankie hates this but the Zoltan part of him seems stronger when in proximity to Georgina and her dad and Zoltan loves this. Frankie feels the dog's pain, the agony of its arthritic joints, the exhaustion in its old muscles and bones.

All Zoltan wants to do is be swaddled in blankets and sleep, which is a blessing for Frankie as he's able to take control of the situation.

He scours the house for inspiration, needs to find out where that thing he conjured and the weirdo clowns have taken Tommy, and the answers, he decides, must be on Georgina's laptop. He knows all of her login details, who

would hide their passwords from their dog, but it's not until he's nosing around her bedroom whilst she's at work that he finally thinks of a way he can use it.
A pencil.

Frankie holds the pencil inside his long narrow, dachshund mouth, and uses the eraser like a makeshift fingertip to switch it on. It's clumsy as hell but he manages to type in Georgina's login details and get online. Frankie's pleased with himself and what he's achieved but he always has the tendency to get carried away whenever he learns a new found skill. After much searching and painstakingly slow typing, he discovers that there is a circus in the local park currently performing and sees the thing's face for the first time in five hundred years.
It's the perfect disguise, a clown, something that can be adjusted and tweaked whenever it sees fit.
Boinky.
At least it has a name now.
Frankie shudders when he recalls the hours he spent in that cellar teaching the blank monster how to torture, maim and kill. Things have come to a head and he is scared of what five hundred years have done to the entity. But he must make contact.
They've taken his only hope to transfer into another human.

It's after he's found out where they are, and he's trying to find out how to turn the laptop off that he sees a sign saying 'voice to text' and wonders if the computer has the ability to do the reverse. When he realises it does it feels like all his prayers have been answered. Frankie points his pencil at the keyboard and begins to practise.

FRANKIE SAYS DIE

Georgina sighs when she sees her dad asleep on the sofa at two o'clock in the afternoon. He's not shaved in days and that means all other personal hygiene rituals have probably been jettisoned too. There's an indentation on the blankets that cover him where Zee usually would be lying and she naturally wonders where her dog is. There's no sign of him in the kitchen.
She hears a noise in her bedroom.
Zee can never muster the energy to battle the stairs nowadays and with the recent shenanigans she's more than a little wary. She focuses on her kickboxing knowledge and sets foot on the first step.
That's when she hears a robotic voice say, "Hello."
"What the fuck?" she whispers and continues to climb despite every nerve in her body telling her to run and that maybe her dad isn't really asleep beneath the blanket.
She takes out her phone and gets the nines up ready to dial but carries on towards her room.
I'm sure I left my door closed.
She knows she did. The rule in their house was that Zoltan wasn't allowed unsupervised in any carpeted room in case of accidents.
She hardly ever opens her curtains either and can see the glare of her laptop on the walls.
"Hello," came the automated voice once more. Heart pounding away in her throat, Georgina edges towards the doorway.
"My name is—"
"Zoltan!" Georgina gasps in surprise at the same time the computer says something else entirely.

MATTHEW CASH

Her dog spins around from the laptop screen looking guilty as fuck, a rubber-tipped pencil falls from his mouth onto her bed.

They stare at one another for a very, very, long time. Neither move, both want to pretend none of this happened. Then Georgina slowly enters the room and looks at the laptop screen. A blank cursor waits for input. She can't believe what she saw, what she heard, so she picks up the dog-slobber covered pencil and hands it back to Zoltan.

After making a lot more eye contact than is normal he reluctantly takes the pencil in his mouth.

"Do it again." Georgina whispers breathlessly and watches in disbelief as her little dog uses the pencil rubber to tap at the letters on the keyboard.

"Hello," the computer says, "my name is," he looks at her, his little beige eyebrows arch in what looks like guilt, and he's back at the keys, "Zoltan."

The floor rushes up and hits Georgina firmly on the arse and a change takes over Zoltan and he jumps off the bed like he's just that moment seen her and comes to greet her with licks and nose-presses.

FRANKIE SAYS DIE

Chapter Thirty-Nine

He's in a cage. Judging by the dung heaped in the corner Tommy thinks it belongs to a lion.
The strong clown sits outside the cage just staring at the inside of the tent. He hasn't moved or said a thing since they got there.
Tommy's cold, hungry and thirsty. At his feet is a battered thermos flask of what he suspects and definitely smells like, the female clown's breast milk. He'd rather die of starvation and thirst if his only options are lion shit and that.
Every so often one of the other clowns comes in to pry, mock, or simply stare at him like he's some exhibit, but never Boinky.
He knows what they are, they're Boinky's changelings, and remembers the tales that Captain Flimbo would tell him of Boinky's origins. They weren't demons as such, not in the sense people think, but survived off the fear of others. Tommy doubts that that's why he's here though.
Boinky was always fond of Tommy, it was he who had turned a blind eye the night he escaped, clamping his arm over Captain Flimbo's bulging man-boob eyes and pointing for him to go.
He knew why he was here. He suspected Greenfield Circus hadn't been as much of a success since his departure and that Ray naturally wanted him back. Well he wouldn't read for them again, wouldn't read for anyone again. Tommy

slumps against the bars and lets gravity pull him to the floor.

Norman slides across the concrete on his buttocks using his hands. He pulls on the thick dust sheet covering his pride and joy. The purple Harley Davidson is still in pristine condition, the only work he has done on her in the last ten years is starting her up and cleaning her.
When he got too doddery to ride any longer people told him to sell her but he couldn't, wouldn't.
He runs his fingers over the name painted on her fuel tank. Demon.
Demon was like a wife to him, and had been a loyal companion throughout his time with The Wasters. But things are coming to an end and he has a new wife to care about.
Norman grabs his toolkit and gets to work.

FRANKIE SAYS DIE

Chapter Forty

Now Frankie's been rumbled he sits back and lets Zoltan take over whilst he contemplates his next move. Georgina's just discovered her doggy is a fuck load more intelligent than she ever gave him credit for and he really doesn't know how to play this.

Georgina's dad doesn't really listen, believe or care as she raves on and on about what she caught Zoltan doing on her bed and Frankie can't really blame him. The poor guy has just lost the love of his life and his daughter, who Frankie is suspecting is short of one or two chromosomes, is more interested that she caught her daft dog browsing the internet than her own mother's, horrible, death.

She spends an hour trying to get Zoltan to perform this self-taught trick in front of her bereaved dad to no avail. All the dog does is chew on two pencils and get one nearly stuck in his throat. That worries Frankie somewhat and he nudges Zoltan aside to take over the driving seat. There's no way he's doing this trick in front of anyone but Georgina, at least then, if no one else witnesses it there's a chance it can be blamed on her being crazy. He waits until night time and they're in her room, her on her laptop as usual.

He picks up the pencil and she excitedly opens the text to voice app.

She's transfixed as he taps away at the keys.

"Hello Georgina," the artificial voice reads his words.

Georgina's hand flutters to her chest, she looks towards the door and is about to call out to her dad.
"No," Frankie types.
Georgina stops herself and looks at the dog she's known for a large amount of her life. "You want this to be a secret?"
"Yes."
"Oh my God, I can't believe this is happening. This can't be real. Can all dogs do this?"
Frankie taps away. "It's real. I'm the only one who can do it."
"But how?"
Frankie knows he can't tell her the truth but whatever he says is going to be equally far-fetched. He stops whilst he considers which would be the least ridiculous out of a government experiment or alien abduction when he decides to go with the almost truth.
He taps away as fast as he can, he's got this pencil typing down to a tee now and watches her face as the robo-voice tells her the how.
"I used to be a man, in my previous life. I don't remember anything about who I was but I know I used to be a man."
"Oh my fucking God, just like in James Herbert's Fluke."
Frankie has no idea what that is but it sounds like he's saying the right kind of bollocks to her.
"And it's taken you this long to find a way to communicate with me." She picks him up and hugs him to her chest before she stiffens. "Umm, how long have you been aware of this? I mean has it happened recently or...?"
"I've always known."
Something about the way Georgina's face falls tells him she's done things she shouldn't have done in front of the dog.

FRANKIE SAYS DIE

"Even that time when I forgot to shut you out of the room whilst I had a w—"
"Yes."
He stares at her for as long as he can, taking immense pleasure in how embarrassed and awkward she feels. He continues his message whilst she sits and wallows in shame.
"I need your help. Tommy is in trouble."
"Tommy?" Georgina frowns, "the homeless dude?"
"Yes."
A smile spreads across her face. "Oh my God, this is totally Lassie: the next generation. Like, I bet Lassie would figure out how to work text-to-speech if she was around in the present day. She'd be able to type stuff like 'Tommy has fallen down the minesh—"
"Lassie is a cunt."
Georgina snorts. "I can't believe you made it swear."
"Tommy has been abducted by clowns."
"Clowns?"
"Yes."
"Wait. Why were you with Tommy?"
"He's Clare buoyant."
Georgina laughs, "You mean clairvoyant. Jeez, Zee, you need to learn to spell."
"I'm a dog."
"Who can communicate with humans?"
"Only you."
"Great. You've shattered my dreams of becoming rich and famous. So Tommy can hear your thoughts, yeah? Knows you're a man trapped in the body of the most adorable dachshund in the world?"

"Yes."

"Okay, so tell me what you know about Tommy's abduction. Oh wait, one thing, if you've been a man trapped in the body of a dog this whole time why the hell have you sniffed so many other dogs' butts and are always nose-diving every piece of shit we walk past? And that dog you mounted the other day. What are you, some kind of pervert?"

Oh Shit, Frankie thinks but doesn't type it. "Keeping up appearances?"

FRANKIE SAYS DIE

Chapter Forty-One

Ray wonders who the pale, elven girl is that floats above Tommy's head. Her image is so vivid that this has to be the wraith of someone still alive. Tommy doesn't have any of the vague, transparent emotional spirits that most people have attached to them. Ray finds it hard to believe that there really is no one long gone that he thinks about and is surprised that one who has been homeless for so long is so besotted with someone, not that those bereft of somewhere to lie their head are lacking in emotion.

When Tommy was abandoned as a child there were constantly two faceless apparitions floating behind him, his parents Ray suspected, but as the lad grew older their images faded. But who is this girl that he thinks about so much?

Almost everyone has their ghosts, often family members will have multiples of the same person. Boinky carries a bunch of these souls around like real balloons, Gormless Pete, Glad Harry, Mr Rapey, Farmer Spacklecock, Albatross Steve and a clown unfamiliar to Ray. Ray knows that some of these people who are still imprinted in Boinky's brain are dead, saw it happen with his own eyes during Clifton's attack. The souls of the dead don't gather around the living, as much as the sentiment brought joy and happiness to people, Ray knew they were chained to their earthly bodies, their rotting carcasses weighing them down like anchors. Destroy the body, free the spirit.

MATTHEW CASH

He walks across the grass and rattles a silver-tipped cane against the iron bars of Tommy's cage. Inside, he wakes up and sees Ray for the first time in decades.

"Hello Tommy."

"Why aren't you dead yet?" Tommy avoids making eye contact.

"That's no way to talk to someone who raised you like their own."

"Last time you saw me you left me for dead."

Ray made no attempt to excuse or deny this. It was true, he found Tommy three months after the circus was destroyed by Clifton and his men and hadn't been too happy. "You brought death on us, nearly ended the circus for good, and then ran away in the middle of the night. What did you expect?"

"I only did what was asked of me. You know how I never had control if I read someone by touching them. A personal object is more than enough and lets me still have control. To be able to withhold the things nobody wants to know. To lie if necessary."

"I made a mistake, and for that I am truly sorry," Ray paces back and forth outside the cage. "You deserved your bodyguards too."

"What do you want?"

"I want you to come back and work with us, Tommy. Things have changed. Changed for the better. My circus has evolved with the new millennium, a phoenix has risen anew." Ray stops directly in Tommy's line of vision. "In a way what happened was for the best. It ended our, let's say, more archaic rituals and performances that are frowned upon nowadays."

"You mean human sacrifice?"

Ray winces. "Magical beings require magical payment."

FRANKIE SAYS DIE

"So everything is kosher now? I don't believe that. Boinky is still here, and he's got a load of friends now."
"Boinky and his children—"
"His children?" Tommy recoils.
"I'm sure you and Captain Flimbo will have a chance to discuss the ins and outs of that now you're back. But all you need to know is that Boinky takes care of his family his way away from the circus."
"But I bet he still takes innocent lives!"
"Things have changed, Tommy, you really would be surprised. I have a new wife, Rochelle, she's a remarkable healer amongst other things."
"And what if I refuse?"
Ray smiles lovingly at big Box, the strong clown. "I guess you can always go and live at Boinky's house. People always love clowns and Boinky's initiation ceremonies have this knack of bringing the most original aspects out of people."
"So that explains Boinky's new recruits," Tommy says with an expression of cold disgust.
"Oh, don't worry," Ray grins, "they were all too young to remember much about the ceremonies, mere infants. I'm sure it'll be a lot more traumatic for an adult."

Ray leaves Tommy to think about his future. He's the only one who's allowed access to the clowns' tent and that's for the best. The days when the Old Acts performed were so hard to cover up. If it wasn't for Boinky's miraculous way at being able to make literally anything disappear they would have got caught decades ago. Ray was just a child himself when the horrors of his father's failing circus drove him to seek help from other parties. Well, they had found him, Boinky and the others. Ray and his father never understood what they really were or where they really came from but once they saw what they could do, the magic, their performances, they knew they could save the circus. Boinky, when he painted himself to look like a more generic clown and stuck his blue wig on was a marvel. His acts of ventriloquism were the best he'd ever seen and he could have the crowds laughing until they almost choked. The others had their specialities. It made Greenfields famous, the best acts in the world.

Boinky takes out thick scoops of white paint and smears it over his head and shoulders and belly. Captain Flimbo muffles incoherently as the makeup is slapped across his face. On a dummy head before him is his fuzzy blue wig. Ray smiles warmly at the clown. "You've always had a thing for that colour haven't you Boinky?"
Boinky turns towards the ringmaster, grins wide and nods. "When he first decided to become a modern clown," Captain Flimbo began beneath the paste, "he wanted to paint the whole of himself blue, like a fucking Smurf."
Ray laughs, "I'm sure he would have made it his own."
Boinky's clowns were all similarly adjusting their costumes, applying makeup where needed. Ray always remembers to treat Boinky with the respect he deserves. He's the last of the Old Acts, his payments for his shows are still the same but since the death of the other five Boinky and his kind get their sustenance in more discreet ways. He doesn't know where Boinky and the clowns go between shows, other that they come and go in that van of his and all he has to do to summon them is think about them. Ray is just grateful they gather their own rewards

unlike the olden days where he and his family would be forced to conspire against groups of schoolchildren, football clubs, sometimes even their last audience of the season. It was Boinky's doing, despite his unusual ways there was a lot more than met the eye to the clown and Ray knows never to underestimate him for that would be a grave mistake.

MATTHEW CASH

Chapter Forty-Two

Georgina doesn't know how to feel about her dog anymore. She's a firm believer in reincarnation and has read umpteen accounts of people remembering smidgens of what they thought were previous existences but she always assumed there was some kind of system reset after your soul got used again. Well there must be. If there wasn't everyone and their uncle Joe would be walking around saying they're some seventeenth century dandy or something. But if Zee has always known...That's kind of creepy.
She remembers when he was a puppy, how she'd let him get in the bath with her and shudders. And that time when I... It wasn't worth thinking about.

The police don't really say much when she tells them about Tommy's abduction, they suggest that it was probably a paid stunt to advertise that the circus was in town. The clowns attracted a vast amount of people during their improv performance in the town centre and no one had reported anything untoward aside from the unfortunate accident involving a taxi and a bus.
Zee doesn't seem to be at all surprised about this news, tells her via the talking laptop that there's something special about Greenfield's clowns, that they're led by someone who is a true master of deception.
"Looks like Velma, Shaggy and Scoob will be investigating some killer clowns then," Georgina ponders. Zee picks up

his pencil, the trick has gotten tedious very quickly, and starts tapping at the laptop. Georgina reads what he's got to say before the voice kicks in.
"Just get me to Tommy and I'll sort everything out."
"What are you going to do, bite their ankles? Woof at them? Piss a lake on the floor so they slip on it?" Georgina laughs at him.
He growls around the pencil as he pokes at the keyboard. "You'd be amazed at what I can do."
Georgina stifles further laughter and dials Suki's number.

"Yo," Suki answers straight away. "Look, I need to tell you something and your going to think I'm absolutely cra—"
"—Zoltan can talk!"
"Hey, what?"
"He can't actually talk talk but he can communicate by typing stuff into a text-to-speech app."
Suki is silent for a long time. "George, have you been smoking shit without me again?"
"Suke, I'm sober as fuck. Come around and I'll prove it to you."
"This better be something better than what I have to tell you, not some kooky shit like he can just press whatever letter of the alphabet you tell him to or something shit like that?"
"That would still be clever!"
"Yeah, sure, but every dog can probably do that."
"They can't."
"Whatever," Suki sighs. "This had just better be like shit-hot because what I've got to tell you is fucking ground-breaking."

FRANKIE SAYS DIE

"Zee, say 'hello' to Suki," Georgina says plonking the dachshund on her bed and handing him the pencil. He looks at her unsure, refusing to accept the pencil.
"She won't tell anyone," Georgina turns to Suki. "Will you?"
Suki rolls her eyes. She still suspects her mate is trippy as fuck. "My lips are sealed Sausage."
Frankie slowly taps at the keys. "Woof."
Suki sniggers at the sound of the effeminate robotic voice. "Okay, clever trick but you could have chosen him a more masculine voice, there's probably settings."
Georgina is a picture of frustration. "You think it's me, don't you?"
Suki smirks. "Come on, I'm not stupid."
"Ask him stuff then."
"George, for fuck sake, come on. Computers can do anything now. You've probably set up some shit like Alexa on it to answer questions and taught him to poke at the keys with the fucking pencil."
Georgina's furious. "Watch him type." She scowls at the dog. "Show her."
Frankie starts pecking at the keyboard.
"Shi—" Suki begins but Georgina clamps a hand over her mouth.
"Hello, Sucky. We need your help."
Georgina explodes with laughter, the kind that comes totally without warning with added snot-bubbles, from both nostrils. "Hahaha. Sucky."
Suki is flabbergasted. "You've got a bloody dachshund that's able to communicate with you and you're taking the piss out of his spelling?"
"Sorry," Georgina snorts. "Sucky."

"Fuck you," Suki punches her in the arm and Georgina shoves her back onto the bed and pulls one of her Converse off.

"Twat," Suki shouts and attempts to pinch where she thinks Georgina's nipples are. She misses by a centimetre on the left side but gets the right one dead on. They're oblivious to Frankie's rapid typing until the artificial voice talks.

"Unless you've both going to get naked, can you please grow the fuck up!"

Chapter Forty-Three

Boinky is sad. It's really hard being an entity that's so mysterious that even he doesn't really know what he is. One moment he just wasn't, the next, he was. Standing in front of six men, not really understanding what they were, where he was, or why any of it was happening. And then the information came at him, fried his brain before it had a chance to turn itself on properly.
Boinky thinks about that time in the dark a lot. When he shuts his real eyes when his body goes slow and he needs what Captain Flimbo says is 'sleep' he sees it over and over again. The men in the air. He remembers feeling little parts of his insides fly from his mouth and go inside them whilst he sucked bits of them out. He doesn't understand what happened, only that Captain Flimbo says it was how he could make friends. The others weren't the same as him because they were inside the people that live in this world, picked up a lot of the trash they left inside their brains when he sucked them out. That's what the Captain says. That's why they were able to blend in, learn better. Captain Flimbo repeatedly tells him this place is called Earth. Boinky liked it best when they all got to be themselves for the night even though the Earth people didn't like their games or having their insides played around with and turned into funny things. Boinky doesn't really understand the concept of death, Captain Flimbo says it's when someone goes away and never comes back. He says that all the Old Acts are dead and never coming back but Boinky

saw their little red stars leaving the men they lived in when the men with the guns shot everyone with their sticks and then he put what looked like one of those little red stars into each one of his clowns.

It was one of the dwarves who saw the four vans turn up in the middle of the night. Little Bobby had been outside walking his rottweiler Santa when they parked up at the edge of the circus ground. Bobby saw the suits and the coats and knew straight away these people weren't police, and when they took shotguns from those long coats that confirmed it. He rushed to Ray's quarters and told him leaving Santa to roam free and attack as many as he could. Boinky was sitting atop the helter-skelter when they came, saw the vans, the men, saw the sparks come from their guns, saw Santa go down as soon as they saw him running towards them.
At night sometimes, especially after the Big Feed, he liked to sit under the stars, watch them twinkle and wonder about what was out there.
Captain Flimbo told him a story once, all about a thing that came from the stars to Earth and disguised itself as a clown to scare and eat children. Boinky liked children, they were funny and special, particularly before they were ruined by the grown-up people. When they had their own special movements and language that was more than words. They didn't have half as much flavour as the grown-ups, the grown-ups were seasoned with all manners of spicy things. Boinky liked the story though and it made him question his own origins and whether he came from somewhere up there too. He was thinking about that when the attack began.

FRANKIE SAYS DIE

The men set fire to the tents and began to shoot everything that moved. Boinky saw a sleek black car pull up and Jeremy Clifton climb out.
Boinky slid down the freshly waxed helter-skelter slide.

On his way across the grass he saw the men throw a petrol bomb through Mr Rapey's caravan window and the magician come raging out of the caravan naked and covered in blood. It probably wasn't his own at that point. He probably still had one or two of the rugby crowd in there as Boinky heard screaming coming from the burning mobile home.
Mr Rapey's eyes lit up with the red star that Boinky put inside him when he was Lord Rapier, he managed to crush the wind pipes of two of Clifton's men before another of them put his gun against his head and blew it away. Rapey's red star came buzzing out of him but Boinky was too busy running towards Clifton, Captain Flimbo wibbling furiously and screaming obscenities.
Clifton looked petrified at the sight of the twenty-five stone, bizarrely-tattooed naked clown running towards him, even more so when his men fired at his sizable bulk and the ammunition did nothing. Boinky struck out with hands and feet, twisted, pulled, snapped and broke until there was just him and Clifton. He could hear commotion in the background, knew he couldn't waste much time with the gang lord but Clifton's future flashed at Boinky just like it flashed at Tommy and the clown was temporarily shocked at what even humankind was capable of. He also saw Clifton's crimes past, present and future, although immediate future as he hadn't got much time left

at all. With all his men down the younger generation of hoodlums would move in like cats on an elderly mice. They would do things far worse than what Boinky could do, and they would revel in it.

Boinky stopped, reached a hand out to Jeremy Clifton's face, pressed his nose with his finger and made a honk-honk noise. Captain Flimbo cackled, he too would have seen Clifton's future, and Boinky ran off to try and save the others.

But he was too late.

As he passed Spacklecock's stables they were already aflame and three of the red stars were zipping above the dancing fire. Mr Rapey's buzzed around his head like a morbid firefly.

Boinky opened his huge mouth and screamed a silent roar of rage and raced in the direction of his remaining friend.

The sight of the men storming Albatross Steve's lighthouse would never leave Boinky's strange brain, there seemed to be too many of them. Albatross Steve climbed to the top of his perch ready to take wing when the men appeared and filled him full of holes before he had a chance to fly. As Albatross Steve's lifeless body sauntered to the ground Boinky just slumped to the ground, opened his mouth and let the black hole inside him swallow the lighthouse and the men and send them to wherever it was he came from.

He swallowed the red stars just like he had puked them up in the first place and with each clown he made he blew a little red star inside them. Like a heart.

So maybe the Old Acts weren't really dead. Maybe they are different because their new bodies were babies when he rehomed them. He has his reservations about his own

FRANKIE SAYS DIE

parental skills but so does every parent. But laughter is the best medicine and he wants his children to be happy and healthy. They got some food from the people in the town but he knows they're ready for something more substantial.

Boinky runs his thumb along Jonathan, his big butcher's knife. Boinky likes to name everything he loves. Bleedy juice comes out of his thumb. There was lots of bleedy juice when the naughty men deaded the Old Acts. With all the excitement about getting Tommy back he can feel that his clowns are hungrier than usual and knows he is going to have to take them out for something to eat. Even Jonathan glints with the anticipation of getting to tickle people's insides ahead of schedule.

MATTHEW CASH

Chapter Forty-Four

"What are you up to in there?" Gloria says, poking her head around the garage door.
Norman is on the floor tinkering with his mobility scooter. "I'm nearly finished."
She walks into the garage, the floor is covered in immaculate Harley Davidson pieces, they're wrapped and labelled like a serial killer's trophies. "Surely the bike would have fetched a lot more money complete?"
Norman grins at her from behind oil-smeared glasses. "That it would have been, that it would have been, but I've used parts of it to make...umm slight alterations to the scooter."
"Slight alterations, using Harley Davidson parts?" Gloria sees a jumble of shining chrome below the scooter's seat.
"In a nutshell, Gloria, I've adapted my scooter to have a 1200cc engine." He points to a motorcycle helmet which rests on its seat, Viper is painted on it in green lettering. "I'll need to wear that when I use it."
Gloria sits on a garden chair and stares at him dumbfounded. "And why is that necessary?"
Norman pushes his glasses up his nose and looks sheepish. "It will hopefully go quicker than the average mobility scooter. I've had to make adjustments to the rest of it too."
"Why the hell do you need a mobility scooter to go that quick?"
"I don't want you to worry but there's something I have to do."

Gloria nods. "Okay, is it to do with the motorcycle club you were in?"

Norman's eyes go wide. "Yeah, yes. Yes it is. A few of the remaining members want to prove that they're not dead yet."

Gloria smiles awkwardly and his face falls.

"Sorry, that was tactless of me." He scoots across the floor and grabs her hands. "Just trust me on this, Gloria. Nothing will come between us and this is just something I've owed someone for a long, long time."

She squeezes his hands rightly as tears form in her eyes. "What's this really about, Norman? Don't lie to a dying woman."

Norman takes his glasses off and rests his head on her thigh and tells her the truth.

"It's congenital I'm afraid, Norman, you said your father passed away when he was..." The doctor studies a sheet of handwritten notes on his desk like even he can't decipher his own scrawl.

"Forty-five," Norman fills in the blank and runs his fingers through his long hair.

He's not even thirty and been told he's got a dicky ticker. He's livid to say the least. Norman leaves the doctor's surgery and gets on his motorbike and drives it as fast and as recklessly as he can home. When he's back at his flat he slams the latest Iron Maiden album into the tape player and cranks the volume up full blast. "Fuck the neighbours, " he screams to his trashed living room. His next door neighbours, two octogenarians knock on the partitioning wall almost in time Nicko McBrain's drum beats. It's okay for them, they've lived twice as long as he probably will.

FRANKIE SAYS DIE

Norman drinks and rages and drinks some more before hitting the local rock pub The Trough.

The Trough is heaving with hair, denim, leather and beer. What he needs now is a decent rock chick to screw his thoughts away, get blind drunk and wake up with a stinking hangover and pretend none of what the doctor said was true.

Tracey-with-the-Tits is behind the bar and all the lads are clawing at the wooden top to get her attention and to get lost down that grand canyon of hers. Norman knows he doesn't stand a chance with her and is more taken by the more flat-chested barmaid that works there who, to differentiate, everyone refers to as Tracey-without-the-Tits. There are many other differences but when T-with-the-T's is in your face there's not a lot else you notice.
Norman goes to his Tracey and she's already taking the top off a bottle of brown ale for him.
"What are you doing in here tonight, Norm? You should be with the lads."
He slaps coins on the counter and downs half the bottle in one. "Didn't feel like it tonight, bab. Wanted to come and look at you instead."

A few hours later they're back at his flat and Tracey-without-the-Tits is naked on his bed looking better than he could have ever imagined and he's kneeling between her legs with his limp dick in his hand crying like a baby. She cradles him like one after he tells her what's wrong, and they sleep in each other's arms.

MATTHEW CASH

"They'll be other times," she promises with a kiss when she leaves the next morning but two hours later is mowed down by a lorry on her way to work.

Good job it wasn't Tracey-with-the-Tits, most people said. Norman breaks completely, socially isolates himself, sells his bike and buys a black Robin Reliant. He's bitter, intoxicated, waiting to die.

That's when Greenfield's Circus comes to town and he catches a glimpse of what they really get up to behind zippered tents. Scores of people being tortured and consumed by other worldly beings. They should have killed him when he saw but they didn't, they took him to their ringman.

That's when Ray Greenfield first let him try his witch doctor juice.

"I should probably be dead by now."

Gloria knows he's telling the truth but finds it all so insane. She tells him as much.

"You'd be surprised at what's out there, Glo. There is stuff in this world that people would never believe even if it jiggled about in front of their eyes."

"You're starting to sound like one of them covid-deniers."

"Not all conspiracy theories are bollocks. Why do you think there are so many forbidden places in the world? Like the Vatican vaults. What's hidden in these places?"

Gloria shrugs, "Valuable stuff? I wouldn't know."

Norman nods, "Yes, but not valuable in the obvious sense. There's stuff in there that'd rock the world, you mark my words."

"Maybe," Gloria appraises the souped-up mobility scooter. "Why do you need it to go so fast?"

Norman's eyes sparkle. "It's a getaway vehicle."

FRANKIE SAYS DIE

"A getaway vehicle? Oh, Norman, what are you going to do, rob a bloody bank?"

"No," he says clutching her hands even tighter, "I'm going to steal Ray Greenfield's flask of voodoo juice and save your fucking life."

FRANKIE SAYS DIE

Chapter Forty-five

They play statues in the corridor. They're good at being still. Boinky peeps through the glass on the door at the crowd inside. Boinky has no idea what the large group of people are doing but likes their pretty flags which they wave over their heads with aggressive vigour.
The town hall is filled to the rafters with them, they wear football shirts, face paints, anything that has that little flag on it, a red cross.
Boinky is selective about what he feeds his children nowadays, likes to think he might be doing this planet he's been living on some kind of justice by getting rid of some of the scum. Captain Flimbo is usually the one who finds these people. Boinky's never been quite sure how Captain Flimbo works, sometimes he's there and other times he isn't, like he can send himself anywhere he wants to at will.
"These lot'll taste good, Boinks, fucking racists always do," Captain Flimbo says excitedly.
Boinky smiles, unfastens the buckles of his dungarees and lets them fall to the floor, he's in his natural state now, naked aside from his filthy ancient tutu.
Captain Flimbo breathes a great sigh of relief at being free in the air.
Boinky's colossal belly-face ripples with anticipation.
Boinky brushes a thumb against Jonathan and his magic knife positively bristles with the upcoming bloodbath.
Boinky beckons Mr Fumble close and points to a door on the other side of the hall and nods at Box. His two sons

make their way around the edge of the hall towards the other door.

"Same routine as usual, Boink?" Captain Flimbo asks. Boinky nods and silently opens the door. He presses his inked-green mouth to Jonathan and four little translucent dragonfly wings sprout along his handle and he buzzes circles in the air. Boinky makes sure Mr Fumble and Box are ready, stands aside and gives the charge signal.

Gnasher and Dave don't even know what they're protesting about. They've been part of this crowd for so many years they've lost track of the politics of it all. But it all amounted to the same thing, fighting, and that was one thing that they loved. Even as lads there was nothing they enjoyed more about a Saturday than the leathering they would give some poor fuckers after the football. It was the best part of the game really. Now they were in their fifties it was more difficult, football violence wasn't so easy to participate in anymore but this kind of thing got the blood pumping just as much.

Someone on the stage was shouting something about homosexuality in schools and how gay teachers shouldn't be allowed to corrupt our children.

"Too fucking right," Gnasher shouts.

"Yeah," Dave is louder and tries desperately to think of a catchy, relevant phrase to get the crowd chanting but nothing is springing to mind. Gnasher looks at him expectantly and he just shouts the first thing he can think of.

"It's School days not school gays!"

Gnasher shakes his head. "That's fucking diabolical, mate."

"I don't see you coming out with anything."

"I'm not a man of words like you Dave."

FRANKIE SAYS DIE

"Yeah well I've lost my mojo, haven't I? Told you we should have gone to the pub first."
Down at the front the rowdy murmur of the crowd changes pitch to horrified screaming.
"Oh, ay up, there might be a brawl instead." Gnasher pushes his way forwards as the crowd surge towards them. They're running from someone with a pink afro, as he gets nearer he sees it's a female clown with gigantic tits. She's totally starkers and she's lunging at people left, right and centre with red fists. Something zips through the air like a rocket, a projectile of sorts, it punches in and out of people in quick successions.
"W-what the fuck?" Dave stammers.
"Clowns, mate," Gnasher states, "Clown terrorists."
Dave begs his brain not try and make a corny joke about what you would call a clown terrorist as he knows it will waste valuable thinking time, something that he doesn't have a lot of.
What do call a clown terrorist?
No, shut the fuck up, Brain, there's people being killed here. Now is not the time.
No, come on, what do you call a clown terrorist?
Please.
More clowns have joined in the massacre. There's one who looks like a pink Incredible Hulk who stands at least three feet taller than anyone else in the room, he's squeezing people's heads like overripe fruit.
What do you call a clown terrorist?
Another who is attacking people with moves like lightning and seems to be able to pick things up with his mind. An assortment of bludgeoning tools surround him, a fire

extinguisher, plank of wood, a brick and they all seem to float about in mid-air.

What do you call a clown terrorist?

Dave is desperate for his brain to quit it. There's another fucking clown entered the hall now and it's got one eye, it's twatting people around the head with an oversized baby rattle and giggling like an idiot. He sees the thing that's flying around get caught in someone's skull and it's a knife. A fucking knife. With wings.

The majority of the crowd are slamming themselves against the main doors, trying to force them open.

Gnasher has up and left him to it and still his brain won't shut up.

Come on, what do you call a clown terrorist?

For fuck sake, Dave gives up and ducks as a decapitated head flies past him. I don't fucking know, Brain, what do you call a clown terrorist?

The main doors burst open and standing there is the most grotesque thing he's ever seen in his life. The clown is naked like the rest of them and, aside from being excessively fat, it's mouth is a wide, stretched, flapping flesh hole. A great big evil looking clown face grins across his belly. He feels the gravity in the building change, flip, and everything, everyone is sucked towards that black vortex. People, furniture, floor tiles all go into the clown's mouth. Dave cries out when his feet begin to slide away from him. His brain is desperate to get its punchline in before he is devoured. His last joke, and it's not even a good one.

What do you call a clown terrorist? A...wait for it...Clunt!

Boinky's eyes glow red as he takes all his children's leftovers away into his forevermouth and smiles as they lick the blood off each other. Jonathan settles in his hand and goes to sleep.

MATTHEW CASH

Chapter Forty-Six

Ray enters the tent. Behind him the strong clown struts his stuff in just a leopard print loincloth. Tommy is disgusted at his cartoonish figure, the little legs look incapable of holding the massive, muscular torso and arms. The clown's face is whited out aside from a comedy straining grin, with added teeth, painted over his lips and chin.
"Somebody skips leg days," Tommy snorts.
"Box," Ray grins to the clown, "please escort The Boy Who Sees to his tent."
"Ray, I told you I'm not doing it. You can't make me read people."
Box pulls the padlock off the cage before Ray can hand him the key and grabs Tommy's wrist in one of his big hands. The clown flips him up onto one of his wide shoulders and leaves the tent.
As they cross the circus ground Tommy can hear the crowds and the funfair.
"You can do it the easy way or the hard way," Ray says. He flicks his eyes up to take in the girl literally on Tommy's mind. "So, are you going to tell me about this woman of yours?"
Tommy appears to be lost in confusion but Ray doesn't think he's got it wrong.
"She's tall, a little too skinny for my liking, looks like she has Scandinavian blood. Has silver hair. I can see why you like her though, she's very pretty. Amazing eyes."
Tommy's reaction says it all.

The clown lets him wriggle and beat at him as much as he likes, it has no effect. "What have you done to her? How did you know?"

"You mean you've forgotten about my own, mostly pointless, gift?" Ray chuckles.

Tommy sags against Box's back. "Don't hurt her. Please. I'll read for you."

Ray smiles and waves a hand towards a nearby tent. Well, that was easy.

"Wait," Tommy calls from Box's shoulder, "What do I do if I see bad stuff?"

Ray's smile takes on a new level of depravity. "Oh, I've moved with the times, Tommy. Everyone of your clients will sign a disclaimer saying that they agree for you to tell them everything you see and will not retaliate for anything they don't like. Plus, Box will be your own personal bodyguard. Did you know, a funny thing, after Boinky's initiation not only did we discover his incredible strength but he's also bulletproof."

"I don't even want to know how you discovered that."

They enter Tommy's tent and just like all those years ago the only thing in there is a small table and two chairs.

"Big opening show tonight." Ray waits for Box to put Tommy down. "If you need anything to take the edge off the side effects of your reading just tell Box here and he'll let me know."

Chapter Forty-Seven

"So, we're going to the circus?" Suki asks as Georgina greets her at the door with Zoltan strapped to her chest in a dog version of a baby carrier.
Georgina nods.
"And what the fuck is that?" Suki says pointing to the dog. "Can't he walk now?"
"Of course he can walk, but now he can talk and stuff this will make things easier when he uses his phone app."
Suki rolls her eyes.
"I can't believe you've gotten over it already. What the fuck is wrong with you? This is kind of a big deal."
Suki shrugs. "You know how I am with emotions and shit. Inside I think it's the most miraculous thing in the world but on the outside I'm just meh."
"Something wrong with you."
"Something wrong with you too."
"Do you reckon we were dropped on our heads when we were babies?"
"Repeatedly."

They leave Suki's house and head towards the park. Zoltan hasn't woofed or anything, just dangles there like a stuffed toy, his little legs poking out and his flappy ears going up and down with Georgina's steps.

Frankie feels like a fucking idiot. As if being a dog could get any more degrading than this. He can't wait to take over Georgina. The first thing he'll do is strangle her annoying friend. See how emotionless she is when her windpipe is crushed and her eyes are popping out of her head.

Almost everyone they walk past either laughs or wants to pet him and he can feel the rage building up inside him. The doggy part of him that is refusing to budge now can smell the filth on their hands, dick germs, arse, a combination of different foods and greases. Zoltan loves all that shit but he doesn't.

They join the queue for the ticket booth and an old lady turns and immediately puts her fingers to his face.

Georgina has never heard Zee act so ferociously, he snaps at the old lady's hand and she recoils, falling back into the people in front of her.

"Zoltan," Georgina shouts, "BAD DOG."

Frankie feels the dog's body flop in shame and curses ever letting the dippy critter back in. He needs to find Tommy, then he'll show everyone the real power of words. He fights for control but for some reason Zoltan's presence is a whole lot stronger this close to his mistress. Frankie concentrates on the swell of Georgina's boobs pressing against the sides of his back and wonders whether he should have a bit of fun when he gets in Tommy again. It's been a while, aside from that dog the other week.

Georgina showers the woman with apologies but the woman's determined to get her money's worth from the situation. She looks about her to make sure a scene is well and truly caused and that she has everybody closeby's attention. "That animal should be put down. It's vicious."

FRANKIE SAYS DIE

"You should be put down, you're vicious!" Georgina can not help but retort.
"Yeah, you totally touched him without our, or his consent. You wouldn't like it if we touched you without your consent." Suki is there beside her best mate, ready for the shit to go down.
"Consent? It's a dog," the woman scowls.
Georgina and Suki stare at one another with open mouths.
"He identifies as a human actually!" Georgina blurts out.
All the people around them, apart from the angry old lady, start laughing.
"He..." even as she's saying it she knows it's a mistake, "can talk."
The old woman looks around at her audience and snorts. "I don't know what you pair are on—"
Georgina ferrets in her coat pocket and brings out a thick rubber stylus that's designed to look like a child's crayon. She taps her phone and puts the stylus in Zoltan's mouth. "Show her, Zee."
The stupid bitch, Frankie thinks, he can't just perform his magic trick in front of all these people. He starts to chew on the thick plastic.
"Aw, look, he's gonna text his doggy friends." Jokes start coming from behind the woman.
"I bet he uses her phone for Facewoof."
"I reckon he watches bitches on Bonehub when she ain't looking."
Frankie's anger still hasn't shifted and something is going on inside him that he's really not happy with, he's actually sympathising with the girls. He hates being laughed at, fucking hates it. Frankie shifts the dachshund's body

around in its little carrier and manages to dislodge one of his back legs. Dachshunds may not be the best of dogs, probably fucking useless as a guard dog, but one good thing they excel at is...

Zoltan lets out a strong stream of hot piss directly into the woman's laughing mouth and when Georgina staggers with the shock of it all he gets a good fair share on some of the jokers too, even hits one in the eye.
They stop laughing then.
Suki drags Georgina out of the queue before she releases the laughter that wants to burst from her like the dog's urine.
"Dachshunds have nervous bladders!" Georgina shouts back over her shoulder as they walk quickly away.

"Well thanks for that," Georgina growls at Zoltan. The park is circled by a high red brick wall and a main road, it's just low enough to give the pedestrians outside the perimeter picturesque views of the interior. The girls watch the hordes of people walk by the boating lake along a path that will lead them to the circus ground. Frankie still has the stylus in his mouth, he's not chewing it anymore but he's rumbling low in his throat
"Oh, what? You got something to say now?" Georgina snaps and taps open the text-to-speech app.
Frankie pecks away at the oversized keyboard. "We can't go in that way, it's too obvious. We'll be seen."
"What's up with being seen?" asks Suki.
"Yeah, they can hardly know we're coming to find Tommy." Georgina shakes her head but remembers something she never asked the dog. "I don't suppose you know why clowns have kidnapped Tommy, do you?"

FRANKIE SAYS DIE

Frankie seizes this opportunity to drop the stylus down a drain they're walking over.

Chapter Forty-Eight

Ray has never seen so many people. For a moment he surveys the crowd with his ghost-seeing eye and the air is thick with spectres. It will be great for his own performance later that evening.
He strides across the circle of sand towards the microphone. Dressed in green, black and red Victorian garb he looks piratical with his long hair and jewellery. He snatches his top hat off his head with a silver-clawed hand and bows to their cheers. His teeth sparkle beneath the lights and his smile is predatorial.
"Welcome to my circus."
He bows again and hears the indoor fireworks explode behind him and music roar as the whole ensemble burst from backstage to prance around the ring, a brief glimpse into what the audience can expect.
Boinky rides out on an oversized go-kart pressing the large red bulb of a massive hooter.
His family come behind him.
Mr Fumble, the more nimble of the crew, walking on his hands and waving his feet, Box is stripped down to dayglo compression leggings and nothing else, his muscles oiled and toned to abnormal proportions. Standing on his shoulders is the heaviest of the crew Libby, the balloonist, she's wearing her best pink dress, the one with daisies on it and her hair is a salmon explosion. The people cry out in a mixture of awe and humour at the giant transparent balloon that floats above her. They look for wires, pulleys,

secrets to how it's all done. Moopy is inside the balloon, his chubby arms and legs kick around at its insides as he waggles his giant rattle in the air.

A plethora of dancers and jugglers cascade across the sand and now there's fire and smoke and explosions as Rochelle makes her debut appearance. There are wolf-whistles galore as they see her for the first time in the flesh, her hair is a braided snake nest of black and green serpents, emerald glitter speckles her ebony skin. She struts towards her husband, her figure-hugging black PVC accentuating every curve, she's a modern-age voodoo priestess, she stands beside him, presses something to her lips and breathes fire at the ground. And standing at the back, just his silhouette seen amidst the smoke, is Tommy. A spotlight illuminates him and as though gaging the audience's reaction to this mysterious suited man Ray announces. "Back after a twenty year sabbatical, The Boy Who Sees. The world's most accurate prophet."

Tommy puts his hands in the air and waves at the hordes of people.

They go wild.

Chapter Forty-Nine

Georgina always knew of the secret way into the park but she always assumed because it wasn't that much of a secret that it would have been cordoned off to stop people gaining free entrance to the circus ground. But it wasn't. She was mega-pissed at Zoltan for dropping the stylus down the drain, it was like he did it on purpose to avoid answering. Both she and Suki searched themselves for something else he could use but neither of them had anything. It shouldn't matter though, they were Shaggy and Velma, the real detectives, Scooby was just the comedy element.

They managed to blend in with the milling crowd as they bundled into the main tent. They followed the others, smiling politely, but keeping their distance, at the affectionate looks Zoltan in his carrier received, and found a place on the rings of benches that circled the arena. Ray came on and the intro commenced. Georgina noticed how Zoltan went stiff as a board when the clowns came out, probably due to the lights and loud noises, but aside from having amazing skills and peculiar quirks, they were just generic clowns to her.
When Rochelle came out both of the girls wanted to come out and Suki even said something along those lines, however a million times more sordid and inappropriate which got her evil glances from the mother of two little

children beside them. Then they saw Tommy and heard what Ray said about him.

"So he used to be part of this," Suki says enlightened.

"It looks that way. He never said anything about it to me."

"How close was your relationship with him? I mean, I know you spoke to him most days, but?"

Georgina shrugs. "I don't know, we only ever talked about stuff that was happening, like, now. I never actually asked why he was living on the streets. I just assumed it was the usual thing."

"But now we know he's The Boy Who Sees and he's been kidnapped by clowns from a circus he once belonged to."

"Hmm, yeah. We need to get to him, talk to him. If he's being held here against his will then we'll have to call the fuzz."

Suki looks like the bottom has dropped from her world.

"Awww. I was hoping we would get chased by a load of clowns and circus freaks. I'd even got a playlist ready on my phone."

"For fuck's sake," Georgina groans with added eyeroll. "Suki, this is real life."

Her mate looks crestfallen.

"Okay, what was on the playlist?"

Boinky couldn't disguise himself from Frankie, no matter how much makeup he slapped on. As the clown sped around and around the ring, waving and pulling faces at the kids, he locked eyes with him and saw the infinite space behind them. Luckily for Frankie there didn't seem to appear to be any kind of recognition on Boinky's behalf. God knows what he might have done then. The laws of black magic don't apply to whatever the clown was, just because Frankie had conjured him didn't mean he could

FRANKIE SAYS DIE

control him. That was how it was supposed to work. You conjure a demon, or a being from the wastelands outside reality, they were supposed to be yours to command.
He wanted nothing to do with the clown or his people, he just wanted that fucking tramp back so he could perform his ritual and get the fuck away.
When Tommy appears at the back he tries his hardest to project himself into him temporarily but there's too much ground between them, no psychic link. He needs to get closer. As the entertainers dispel and the first act gets ready to perform Tommy leaves the ring and Frankie woofs loudly in his direction.

"Well we obviously need to get an appointment with The Boy Who Sees. Do you think he will see us coming?" Suki quips as they leave the audience to watch Mr Fumble juggle an assortment of live power tools.
"Please," Georgina gripes, "now is not the time for jokes of that calibre."

They leave the main tent and head towards a smaller one which has Tommy's stage name on a sign above the entrance. The huge beefcake clown stands outside it with his arms crossed in front of his chest. He looks down at them with piggish eyes and says,"ticket."
The two girls exchange glances, daring each other to be the one to talk.
"Ummm, we don't have one. We're Tommy's friends. Can we just have a word with him? Please?" Georgina asks as politely as possible, giving him her best smile.

MATTHEW CASH

"No ticket. No Tommy," the big clown turns his face away in defiance.

"Okay," Georgina sighs, "where can I get a ticket to see him?"

Box points a finger behind her and forces the words out one at a time, "Ticket. Box. Ray."

Georgina follows his finger towards an open-sided caravan with ticket booth painted on it, but between them and the ticket conveyor strides the ringmaster.

"Good evening my friends," Ray says, showing his silver teeth. He knows instantly who the white-haired girl is, he's seen her apparition floating around Tommy since he arrived. She has none of her own attachments but the oriental looking girl is carrying the spectral form of an old man everywhere with her. Ray suspects grandfather or uncle. There's something odd about the dog, something he's never ever seen before. The animal seems to be blurred at first but then he realises it's because he's looking at two of them, one slightly overlapping the other. Like the dog has had a facsimile imposed over its own body but it's not been lined up perfectly. Ray's intrigued by this discovery but can not afford to waste time trying to mull it over as he senses the girls could be trouble.

"Woh, dude, what's with the eye?" Suki says without any decorum. She moves forward slightly and stares directly at Ray's albino eye and the white streak which runs through his hair. "Is it real?"

Ray smiles and takes pleasure in their fascination over his strange appearance, he runs a hand through his long hair and laughs, giving them a glimpse of his silver capped teeth. "It's the only one of my peculiarities that I was born with but as you can see," he flicks out his tongue, it's split

in two, "I'm into body modifications and all types of extreme artform, so it fits with my image."
"It's so cool." The way Suki says it makes Georgina instantly elbow her in the ribs. She knows exactly how her friend's perverted little mind works, she's probably already thought about the things he could do with that forked tongue. "We would like an audience with The Boy Who Sees, please?"
"I'm afraid he's all booked up this evening," Ray says with genuine concern. "However, if you want to stick around until the end of the night I'm sure we'll be able to figure something out."
"Oh." That wasn't what Georgina was expecting.
"Thanks, Mr Greenfield," Suki's embarrassingly sweet. Georgina is surprised she doesn't curtsey.
"Ray, please," Ray gestures back to the main tent. "Now run along, you don't want to miss the performances." He waits until they're headed away from Tommy's tent and slips through the entrance to see his seer.

Chapter Fifty

"Your first client of the night has arrived."
Tommy's nod is barely perceptible. He slumps on one of a pair of leather armchairs. They seem out of place inside the tent on the grass but at least they're comfortable. "When are you going to let Georgina go?"
"Once I can trust you," Ray says. He deliberately keeps his distance from Tommy, knowing the man's powers. Who knew what he might risk to get information about this girl. If he found out she wasn't his prisoner, yet, he would try and escape again.
"Can I see her?"
"You read for these three clients tonight and I'll arrange something, I promise," Ray spoke with such sincerity it was hard for Tommy not to believe him.
Tommy hangs his head in his hands and sighs. "Three is going to kill me."
"You only have to read every other day. I understand how this affects you. I have access to a whole apothecary of pharmaceuticals to aid your recovery. Whatever I can do, I will do to make you feel comfortable."
"Okay." Tommy knows that's the best he can hope for but as Ray leaves the tent and Box brings his first client in an as yet undiscovered devious element of Tommy surfaces and he realises that he doesn't have to give genuine readings. For the first time in his life he can be dishonest.

MATTHEW CASH

The lady looks familiar but with everything that's been going on Tommy can't recall where he's seen her. He used to see many regular faces sitting on the street begging. She's nervous as she's led by the clown to the other armchair, Tommy smiles reassuringly. "Hello, I'm Tommy. It's okay, I'm sure there's nothing to worry about."

She's stony-faced."No, I want the truth. I paid for the truth, sign all your disclaimers. Be brutal, tell me everything."

It's obvious she's worrying about something, it's etched to her face, deepening her age lines. Tommy wastes no time in any chitchat. "Do you have something personal I can hold to do your reading? It can literally be anything that you touch regularly, a piece of clothing, jewellery."

She fumbles with her handbag indecisively for a moment before pulling a gold band from her ring finger.

Tommy allows her to plop the ring into his palm, it's icy cold. He closes his fingers around it. "Is your partner still alive?"

"You're the fortune teller. You tell me."

Tommy smiles awkwardly. "It's okay, I just wanted to make sure you understood I don't see people who have passed on. I can only see your future."

"He's out in the car park. Hates all this mumbo-jumbo," she nods at Box, "and clowns." Box looks crestfallen. "No offence, like."

"We can't all be the same," Tommy says and closes his eyes in preparation for his first fake reading. He knows the sort of thing this woman will want to hear, she's nearing the time of life where she's going to be frightened about how much time she has left and how able she is going to be whilst she's still here. He'll give her what she wants. Or at least what he thinks she wants. He plots the basic outline

FRANKIE SAYS DIE

of what he plans to say and he'll gauge her reaxtions to see if he's hitting the right buttons.

"You're both still very much in love," he says, studying her every expression. "You and your partner both worry about the other one dying before them but let me tell you something that might come as a reassurance. When it's time for you both to go you will go hand in hand."

The woman gasps and sits back in the chair, she obviously wasn't expecting him to tell her something like that, however after a few seconds the shock settles into a serene smile.

"There's no need to worry about anything, " he forces a laugh, "you live a fast, fun-filled happy life together before then, doing things people even half your age couldn't do." He can tell by how happy she is, he's saying the right things but he knows not to over do it. "Just have fun and follow your heart. Do what you want to do." It was all cliché jargon, stuff that people wanted to hear. There is no way he is going to do genuine readings for Ray Greenfield anymore, he's made that decision. He's going to find Georgina and get away, away from the circus and away from that bloody dog, wherever it is. Tommy hands the lady back her ring.

"Well your boy who can see the future is a load of twaddle," Gloria states as she crosses the gravel car park towards the man on the mobility scooter. It's finished now, the souped-up engine is now hidden beneath a curved metal plate that Norman's sprayed black with orange flames and The Beast Reborn emblazoned across it in red jagged lettering. He's even cannibalised parts of his bike to change the handlebars. It's a mobility scooter any old biker would be proud to ride.

"I don't understand," Norman says. "What did he say?"

"Reckons we've got a fun-filled, happy life together. That we'll die in each other's arms."

A smile splits Norman's face in two and he lets out a joyous laugh. "Don't you see. He's right. This means whatever happens tonight. We'll be successful."

Gloria's frightened but the faith Norman has in the boy is contagious. She wraps her arms around him, ignores the smell of his ancient motorcycle leathers, and plants a kiss on him.

FRANKIE SAYS DIE

Chapter Fifty-One

"The way Ray has worked out the evenings is pretty cool," Suki says flashing a flyer she's found somewhere in Georgina's face. Georgina doesn't have a chance to look at it or respond before the girl continues. "The circus is like two circuses in one, you've got the main tent, the one where we saw everyone at the start," Suki points at the giant red and green striped expanse in front of them. "And then you've got the grown-ups one over there." On the other side of the field is a smaller version which rears beneath a large tree. "That's where Ray's wife, bitch, hosts what looks like a circus of horrors. Fire eaters, sword swallowers and such."

"We're not here for the entertainment, Suke," Georgina snaps irritably. Zoltan's wriggling in the doggy carrier like it's infested with ants. "Look, I think Zee needs the toilet. I guess we can watch some of the shows until I figure out what the hell we're going to do."

Suki bounces excitedly. "Yass. Let's go to the grown-up tent and see how amazing this wife of his is."

Georgina unfastens the harness and puts Zoltan on the grass.

"It's funny," Suki says as the dachshund scurries around, nose brushing the freshly cut greenery, looking for somewhere to go, "for someone who thinks they used to be a man, there are times when he just acts like a dog."

Georgina hates to admit that her friend has a point. "Yeah, you'd think he'd just find somewhere where no one's looking and just do it but aside from him showing us he can communicate, he has pretty much just acted like a dog his whole life."

"Hmm," Suki says as the dog zigzags back and forth. "There couldn't be a chance he's lying, could there?"

"You've seen him type!"

"I have. But what's to say he's telling us the truth?"

"Woh," Georgina recoils, offended. "Are you calling my dog a liar?"

"Not as su—"

"Are you calling my bloody dog a liar?"

"Yes," blurts Suki and she clamps her hand over Georgina's mouth before she has a chance to complain any more. "Listen, there's some stuff I was reading about online about soul transference."

"What the fuck are you on about now?"

"There are ancient rituals that are rumoured to enable you to put yourself in someone else's body. Like body swapping except you just take over the other person like some parasite. I don't know what happens to the host."

Georgina rolls her eyes. "You trying to say someone zapped themselves into Zoltan? Why?"

"Not on purpose."

"Oh so what, they sneezed whilst eating a fucking kebab and accidentally say the words to some black magic juju and—"

"Livers!"

"Did you just scream 'livers' at me?"

"Yes."

"Why?"

"Some used to think eating other people's livers allowed that person's spirit to live on in them."

"You totes should have said 'liver on in them' then, that would have been hilarious."

FRANKIE SAYS DIE

"I'm being serious George."
"Can I be Crazy Suki?"
"Stop taking the piss," Suki shouts and for the first time ever Georgina actually believes she's being serious.
"I think The Smiler tried to transfer himself into you by force-feeding you part of his liver, but—"
"Zoltan ate it," Georgina cuts in, suddenly seeing the light. "Oh my fucking God. You think that a serial killer has possessed my fucking do—"
Suki grabs Georgina's arm. "Where's he gone?"
Apart from people moving from one tent to the other there is no sign of the little dog at all.

MATTHEW CASH

FRANKIE SAYS DIE

Chapter Fifty-Two

Matt Humphries isn't the owner of Humphries' Everyday Essentials, he's not even related to whichever Humphries it was that started the chain of hardware stores, but he does work for them, has one of the weirdest jobs ever in fact. Whenever he tells people what he does for a living they don't usually believe him. He's the chief taster for Humphries' Everyday Essentials dog food. It's not half as disgusting as it sounds and since new rules and regulations came into play pet food now has to be fit for human consumption too. Sometimes he even gets to don the chef's hat and create new recipes.

He loves his job, loves animals.

He walks towards the tiny tent full of anticipation. The disclaimer he had to fill in was a novel it was that big. He only briefly scans it but the basic gist is, he won't complain about what the fortune-teller, or whatever the proper term is, tells him. He doesn't really give a shit, isn't a believer of this nonsense anyway but sometimes going to see these folk help shape him where future decisions are made. Mostly he only asks them about his business ventures, he refuses to listen to anything personal, that's where they get you, that's where the worry starts. He's not interested in health or love, just how he's going to make his first million. He sucks on a device that looks like some kind of futuristic musical instrument and releases plumes of aniseed-scented grey vapour from his nostrils. It helps to take the smell of Humphries' Choice Chunks off his breath.

MATTHEW CASH

He's shown into the tent by a great big bastard of a clown who's acting as the mystic's bouncer. Matt didn't know what he was expecting, hadn't seen any pictures of The Boy before and didn't arrive in time to see the circus performers at the start, but the man in the tent isn't it. He's too thin, too ordinary looking to be someone who can tell the future, and there's no paraphernalia about like there was with the pier prophet, just two chairs and that's it. He can't help but feel a little bit let down. "I was expecting candles and a crystal ball," he half-jokes as a way of entry. The Boy Who Sees gives a lukewarm smile at his humour and stands up to greet him. "All that stuff is for charlatans, I'm the real deal."
Matt offers Tommy his hand to shake. "That's what all the charlatans say too."
Tommy laughs genuinely at this and gestures for the man to sit down. "Do you have something personal, something you always carry about yourself, that I may hold to perform your reading?"
Matt thinks for a moment and offers him his vape pen. "Will this do? It rarely leaves my hand."
"Of course," Tommy nods but when he reaches his hand out to take the device Box's big paw snaps around his wrist.
The giant clown lowers his face level with Tommy's and he looks into the clown's black eyes. "No, cheating," he says in neanderthal grunts.
Tommy can feel the bones in his wrist grinding together. "I wasn't going to—"
Box's eyes bore into him. "No headache with the last one. You lied."

FRANKIE SAYS DIE

Tommy has underestimated the clown, and didn't think any of Boinky's lot would have anything much in the brain department.

"Hold his hand," Box demands Matt. The dog food taster seems a little shaken by the sudden sinister turn of events and his hesitation sees how far Box's patience runs. He grabs hold of Matt's wrist yanking both men out of the armchairs and mashes his palm against Tommy's and pins them together inside one giant fist. "Now, read!" Box roars at Tommy so loud he feels the pressure of it against his eardrums.

"Do it, for fuck sake," Matt says scared as fuck and Tommy does for his sake.

Chapter Fifty-Three

Frankie slips under the tent material without being noticed and for the first time since landing himself in this situation he's grateful for the daft little dog body. The big clown has got Tommy and some bloke on the floor, now would be a perfect time to bodyswap for a spell of mindless violence but Frankie knows he wouldn't have a chance in hell against that fucking thing. It's like someone's painted a clown face on a gorilla. All he can do is huddle in the shadows and wait for Tommy to do his reading.

Tommy grimaces at the sudden eruption of pain in his head and the horrific graphic imagery that sears across his mind. He has no choice other than to tell the man what he sees, it's beyond his control. "It's disgusting. Disgusting. Big, metal teeth. Red eyes. Churning, mincing death, so much meat and offal." He stares at the man in abstract horror. "What the hell are you going to do?"
The man, however frightened, chuckles. "I make dog food, mate. Sounds like your seeing the mincer where we chuck all the ingredients in."
Tommy shuts his eyes, knows there's no choice than to let the reading run its course. He makes sense of the bizarro inside his head and sees that, yes, it is a machine, red eyes are buttons, lights. Silver cans stick, like flies on flypaper, to a long black conveyor belt, which he mistook for a gigantic tongue. Something squirts a foul-looking paste into the tins as they roll along and the scene changes to a

stocked shelf in a shop with the word new above it. He laughs through the pain, through his over dramatic reaction to something so mundane. "I think you're going to create a new flavour of dog food."

"Is that it?" Matt says majorly disappointed.

Tommy sees the stuff flying off the shelves. "It's a big seller," he adds like it's some kind of consolation.

The pressure in Tommy's head begins to rise and the images he sees cloud over. "I'm sorry, that's it. That's it," he screams up at Box who releases the two men. Tommy falls to the ground.

"Are you alright, son?" Matt asks Tommy. Tommy doesn't answer so he asks the clown the same question.

"He's okay," Box says and gently pushes Matt towards the exit, "just resting."

"Are you sure?"

"Yes, I get him parrots eat them all," Box says trying his best to reassure the man.

"What?" Matt stops and stares dumbfounded at the clown.

"Parrots eat them all," Box repeats and taps a finger to his head. "For his headache. You have aches in the head, you get the parrots to eat them all."

"Paracetamol?"

"Yes, yes," Box grins with wide excitement, happy that Matt finally understands him. "The parrots will come to eat the pain."

Matt shakes his head. This is obviously some clown humour that is far above, or below, his intelligence. Still, it doesn't matter, it's not been a completely wasted trip. He walks out of the tent with thoughts about dog food.

Frankie watches from the shadows. The man and the clown leave Tommy to lie in a semi-comatose stupor.

FRANKIE SAYS DIE

Without any further hesitation he slips out of Zoltan's body and into Tommy's.
From the second he's inside he knows his powers over the lad are weakening. His presence hasn't automatically shunted Tommy's out and he can sense him still rattling around in there with him. Thoughts of dog food factories and rescuing Georgina still fill his mind and Frankie feels the intense agony that Tommy's readings cause.
Fuck this, he thinks and tries to zip back into the dog but when he tries to do that he sees the bloody thing has run off and remembers due to his weakening state and close proximity to Georgina he hadn't been able to shed the dog's soul completely either which meant the dog would be back to its normal self.
From outside the tent come the sounds of Box stomping across the grass and a strange, ethereal screeching.
Frankie tries to force Tommy's body to sit up but it's like he's had a stroke or something, there's no control. He manages to roll onto one side just as Box comes in with a huge birdcage.
"Got parrots eat them all, Tommy."
Frankie feels genuine fear when he sees the flurry of movement in the cage. Box lowers his fingers to the door's catch and whatever is inside settles. There's three of them and they are definitely not parrots. Oh, they have wings, of sorts, but they're more like the flayed orange skin of something that's been torn asunder. Ripped dragon wings, that's what they look like and they drip with a purple substance that seems to leak from the creatures' pores like sweat. Their bodies are covered with the same mottled orange skin and they are oval in shape. Instead of feathers,

needle-fine spines like porcupine quills. Their heads are like an A I simulation of a hybrid between a bird, reptile and something from the dark trenches of the sea, completely featureless apart from twin black holes side by side. When Box opens the cage Frankie hears the horrible screeching again and expects to see those little holes pucker or gape but the creatures are making the noises by rubbing a collection of red, grasshopper-like legs together hidden in their unnatural plumage. One by one they leap from the cage and come towards him. Frankie desperately tries to make Tommy move but he just can't.

The first of the birds lands on his chest and two long pink proboscis shoot from the holes in its head and latch on to his forehead. Frankie instantly feels Tommy's pain begin to subside and watches the bird grow fatter and blush red. The other two join their friend and Box smiles down at his feeding pets. "Parrots eat them all."

FRANKIE SAYS DIE

Chapter Fifty-Four

Laughter is so much tastier than fear, Boinky decides, but it has to be that genuine kind where the laughee has no control or care over what they look or sound like. The sort of laughter that makes people grab hold of their bellies like they're being gutted and snot bubble-pop from their noses and they explode in a cacophony of hiccups, burps, whoops and wheezes. That type of laughter was far more settling on his tummy than anything else. People's screams of terror were just a temporary fix, junk food, whereas true laughter could fill him up for days. He knows his children are very young but hopes that he can train them to find sustenance from the less negative emotions humans have to offer. Joy, happiness, love, laughter, excitement were all just as filling as fear and sorrow and they weren't always so hard to achieve.

He leaves his audience cheering for more. His ventriloquist act always got a good response and they could never work out how Boinky managed to throw his voice so successfully. Captain Flimbo was obviously the brains behind that particular trick, Boinky was just the one who danced around acting the clown drinking in the audience's laughter and happy faces. Children were the best ones, especially the tiny ones. As people got older they became more suppressed like they were scared to show their true feelings. Boinky loved children, that's why he never let his own children eat children. The concept behind his troop's feeding rituals were that they consumed their prey when they were at their peak point of a particular emotion. It was unfortunate that fear was the easiest and quickest thing to instil in someone. In real life people were much easier to suddenly frighten than to suddenly make happy. Boinky tried and tried to teach his children that actual physical consumption wasn't necessary but now that they had discovered how tasty the unbridled fear of imminent death was they were like junkies. He had grown-up since the Old Acts played the circus, discovered the nutritional value of making people laugh to the point where they wet themselves, found out just how delicious the taste of festive joy was in the little ones, the children that still believed in magic and fairy tales. There was no need to corrupt and kill, humans did that enough to one another and it had taken him most of five hundred years to learn this lesson and he would teach his clowns it even if it took him another five hundred or if he couldn't he would just lead them all into his forevermouth and send them all back where they came from.

Boinky sits on a stool in the dressing up tent, takes his big blue wig off and starts to unfasten his clown costume.

"What's that?" Captain Flimbo says somewhat groggily as the lights hit him. Boinky turns around but can't see what he's on about so sets about removing the facepaints. Something scurries behind him, he sees it reflected in the mirror and spins around with the grace of a ballerina. Boinky's half uncovered face breaks into a huge grin when he sees what's come into the tent.

"Aw, a little doggy," Captain Flimbo coos. "Don't eat it!" Boinky slaps a hand over his belly, as if he would eat it. He's only physically eaten his children's leftovers since they were born and Captain Flimbo should know that.

FRANKIE SAYS DIE

Boinky crouches down to try and make himself appear less threatening.

"'ello little dog!" Captain Flimbo shouts and the dog jolts in surprise.

Sometimes Boinky wishes the Captain would be as quiet as he was. Boinky stays as still as he can and lets the dog come to him. It's what you do with animals, you have to build up trust. The little dog is nervous at first, three steps forward, five back but eventually it sniffs his hand. Boinky gently picks it up and cradles it in his arms.

"Where did you come from then?"

"Ummm, excuse me, sir?"

Boinky eyes the dog for a second in childlike wonder before Captain Flimbo says, "Over there, you great lummox."

Boinky looks up from the animal and sees two girls standing in the tent. His grin feels slightly awkward.

"You're so good at that," says a girl with dark hair wearing a bright coloured monster hoodie. "Can't even see your lips moving or anything."

Boinky nods and points.

"He likes your top," Captain Flimbo tells her and Boinky puts his thumbs up in agreement.

The girl laughs, it tastes lovely.

"That's, ummm, my dog," the other girl says.

Boinky smiles, pets the dog and places him gently on the grass. The little dog stays by his feet, looking up at him doleful. Boinky plops to the ground, the dog is all over him covering his face with licks, he can't help but laugh as the animal runs amok.

"Aw, he likes you," the dark-haired girl says.

MATTHEW CASH

"He loves animals, does Boinky," Captain Flimbo tells them despite it being self-explanatory.

Sudden shock changes the girls' faces before the dark-haired one grins widely. "Now that is really impressive. How the hell do you manage to talk and laugh at the same time?"

"It's probably some kind of pre-recorded device hidden somewhere," the blonde says trying to hide her awe.

The dark-haired girl can't help but eye Boinky's exposed belly. "Do you have a giant clown face tattooed on your stomach?"

Boinky stops playing with the dog and there's an expression of coy childishness about him.

"Uhoh, Boinko, m'lad, we've been rumbled," Captain Flimbo says with a jiggle.

Boinky gets to his feet and opens his clown costume to reveal his gigantic gut and the face of Captain Flimbo in all his glory.

The blonde girl looks like she's trying to hold back vomit but the dark-haired girl gawps with fascinated astonishment.

"Oh, my fucking God, that is so fucking cool," she says, her eyes taking in every detail of Captain Flimbo's face. "I mean, it's totally fucked up, must have taken ages to get done—"

Boinky proudly stabs himself in the chest with a thumb.

"You did it yourself?"

He nods and grins.

"Dude, you are so fucking badass."

Boinky blushes and waves away her words.

"You'll be giving him a big head."

FRANKIE SAYS DIE

When Captain Flimbo says that Boinky starts to fumble with his trousers before he's interrupted. "Ey, the ladies don't need to be seeing those tattoos, Boink."
Dark-haired laughs, blonde just looks disgusted.
"Can I get a photo with you?"
Boink nods at the dark-haired girl who hands the blonde her phone and stands beside him.
"Make sure you get my good side," Captain Flimbo jokes and Boinky thrusts his gut towards the camera as the dark-haired girl poses beside him.

MATTHEW CASH

Chapter Fifty-Five

"What's going on?"
Box snaps his head around to look at Ray. He whistles and the three Parrots-eat-them-all carefully hop onto his forearm like three grotesque, rubbery balloon-things. Tommy lies unconscious at his feet. "Parrots-eat-them-all," he offers as an explanation.
Ray looks livid at what he assumes is Tommy's corpse. "I told you not to use any of your special methods of healing." He grimaces at the avian monstrosities as Box ushers them back into their cage.
"Tommy have no pain now."
"You've fucking killed him!" Ray shrieks pointing at the ghost that stands over the fallen man.
Box shakes his head so hard Ray hears his cheeks slapping against his teeth.
Tommy slowly opens his eyes and now Ray is more confused than angry.
Why are there two of them?
He crouches down. "Hello, Tommy, can you hear me? How are you feeling?"
Frankie can't talk, the best he can do is smile, nod and stick a thumb up.
"Something's not right here." Ray moves away from Tommy's body and stares at his ghost. "Can you hear me?" It's the first time in decades since he's actually tried to communicate with someone's attached spirit. From his experience though those who are simply a memory that

someone can't let go of do not communicate, can not communicate, they're just a visual, albeit to the trained eye, manifestation of the person on someone's mind, but Tommy's ghost nods. He's taken aback, even more so when he talks to him.
"Ray, you've got to help me."

"So, where do you think this special potion will be?" Gloria says walking beside Norman.
"In his trailer." Norman nods toward the long red and green lorry with Greenfield's Circus on it. "It's just a matter of getting in there." He steers his scooter in that direction and almost ploughs into a man who is vaping so hard he appears to be steam-powered.
"Fucking lunatics," the man mutters through a licorice cloud.
"Oi, who are you calling a lunatic?" Gloria, never one to shirk away from confrontation, steps in his path.
The man thrusts his vape pen at the tent she visited earlier. "Them. Fucking clowns and fortune-tellers."
"Nothing wrong with that fortune-teller, mate," Norman barks from his seat.
"If you say so, but them clowns are fucked," he pauses, sucks and expels white, "I fucking hate clowns."
Norman laughs. "You ain't the only one. I take it they've done you a mischief?"
"You could say that," the man adds and continues towards the car park.

"Someone keeps taking control of my body." If he were to have said it to anyone else they would have laughed at him, well actually, in his present state they probably

FRANKIE SAYS DIE

wouldn't have seen or heard a thing, but Ray just listens. "He says he's a five hundred year old warlock and he's found out how to swap bodies with people by performing a special type of ritual. Thing is, he fucked up and ended up in the body of a dachshund—"
Ray remembers the girls and the little dog with the matching ghost.
"He needs to be able to say the ritual and he can't cuz he's a dog," Ghost Tommy laughs at the stupidity of it all. "That's where I come in. I'm psychic and have a connection strong enough for him to temporarily possess me."

"Okay," Gloria says from the top of half a dozen steps leading up to the door in the side of Ray's lorry. "Keep an eye out and if anyone comes toot the horn on that thing."
Norman nods, slips one hand inside the golf bag that rests where his legs should, and scans the surrounding area. Gloria pulls a hairpin from her hair and gets to picking the door lock, a trick she learnt in her teenage delinquent years.
"How will I know this flask when I see it?"
Norman starts to give her an in depth description of the flask when one of Ray's clowns walks out of a tent in just a pair of baggy trousers followed by two girls and a dog.
"Shit, Glo, stay still." Norman watches the group cross the grass, they're quite a way off and it's getting dark now. "It's okay, I think we're good. Carry on."

MATTHEW CASH

Frankie thinks something suspicious is going on. The ringmaster has suddenly gone silent and seems to be listening intently to something that's directly above him. He can't detect anything from the man but it doesn't take him long to guess he's a medium of some kind and Tommy's ghost is communicating with him. The muscle-clown is bent over him gently coaxing his freak birds back into their care. Frankie knows he needs to make a run for it before Tommy let's the goose out of the net or whatever the fucking expression is. The clown's alien birds have made the body he's in feel like new, invigorated. He slowly pushes himself up onto his elbows and looks at the nearest thing to his face, the clown's dangling gooch.

Ray can't believe what he's hearing. He's heard myths about the liver-eating ritual, his voodoo connections mentioned it but no one knew the secret incantation to put the magic into practice.
"He wants me to recite the mantra and feed his liver to Georgina," Tommy explains. "Help me and I'll stay with the circus. I'll read all you want."
Ray opens his mouth to answer but Box lets out an agonising scream and the cage of Parrots-eat-them-all comes sailing towards him. Ray ducks the flying cage and sees Corporeal Tommy attached to Box's crotch by his teeth. The cage of what-the-fucks explodes on the grass and the floppy birds hop out and attempt flight. Corporeal Tommy lets go of Box's balls, crawls through his legs and legs it out of the tent dragging Ghost Tommy through the air behind him.
Ray jumps up to give chase but hears two girls cry, "Tommy" and Captain Flimbo shout "what the fuck?"

FRANKIE SAYS DIE

"I can't believe it was just sitting there," Gloria says giving the flask a shake to check it wasn't empty.
"He doesn't expect people to know what it is." Norman secrets the flask in his golf bag and Gloria sits across his thighs.
"Come on, let's get out of here."
Norman speeds up a little, kind of disappointed that he's not had the opportunity to push his souped up ride to its limits but knows it's probably for the best, but as they skirt by the tent the clown and two girls went in he hears the sound of an altercation and can't resist eavesdropping. Tommy rushes past him with absolutely no recollection and Norman laughs at the thought of Ray losing his star act.

Boinky doesn't know what's going on apart from the fact that Box is grabbing his bits with one hand and frantically trying to catch his parrots-eat-them-all with the other. The two girls look horrified at the grotesque birds hopping and jumping away from the big clown. Ray clocks them and their little dog and barks orders at Box. "Leave the birds and grab the girls and that dog."
Box snatches a wrist in each hand and the dachshund instantly cowers behind Georgina.
"What's going on, guv?" Captain Flimbo cuts through the sounds of the girls struggling.
"It seems we have a witch in our midst."
Boinky scopes the two captured girls.
"It's not us," Suki snaps, trying to pull away from Box.
"No," Ray says, "according to our seer friend Tommy your little dog there consumed the liver of a five hundred year

old warlock and is the only key he has to achieving some form of immortality."

"Fucking told you!" Suki says with a smug grin.

"Boinky, don't you da—" Captain Flimbo is interrupted mid-wibble as Boinky dives on the ground and grabs the dog in one big hand. Boinky's eyes burn red with unaccustomed anger and his mouth starts opening to unnatural widths.

"No," Georgina yells and kicks at Box to no avail.

Boinky dangles the dachshund over his fast expanding forevermouth, oblivious to the spray of piss the dog rains down on his face.

"Boinky, no!" Ray bellows, "he's not in there yet."

Boinky's fires extinguish and he slowly lowers the animal but refuses to let go. His mouth shrinks back into a facsimile of normality.

"This warlock," Ray starts, "has a bond with Tommy, can temporarily use his body but he needs the dachshund to complete his next bodyswap."

"It's that fucking Foster," Captain Flimbo growls, "after all this time our paths cross again."

"The one who conjured you?" Ray is gobsmacked.

Boinky nods, Captain Flimbo talks. "He set us free in the world but only after brainwashing us to believe the only food here is fear." Boinky gazes tearfully at the girls. "But there is so much more. Humankind is a selection box of emotional treats. Boinky has taught us this over the last hundred or so years. Happiness, laughter, love, are even more toothsome and can last a lot longer." Boinky scowls so hard at Zoltan that he whines. "But it's too late for Boinky's clowns, that's all they know. Fear is the easily sourced junk food for them, everything else is tasteless mush. And it's that evil cunt's fault."

FRANKIE SAYS DIE

Ray can't believe what he's hearing, that this entity from beyond the stars has a soft spot for humanity.
"Whatever you are," Georgina says looking into Boinky's eyes, "it seems that you've taught yourself the difference between right and wrong, good and evil. You are obviously a naturally peaceful being."
"Nah," Captain Flimbo disagrees and then puts her right. "We were a neutral being, shaped by the one who conjured us. That's what Boinky's pissed off about, he wants revenge for the countless lives he and his family have taken when there were other choices."
"So you've learnt compassion?"
"I guess you could say that."
Georgina nods. "Then please, put down my dog and remember that he's still a dog too. Still that little dog I caught you playing with only moments ago."
Boinky's eyes suddenly melt and his lips quiver. He hugs Zoltan to his chest and plants a big wet kiss on his head. Zoltan looks at him in bug-eyed confusion for a second before licking his round face. Boinky laughs and licks him back before gently lowering him to the grass.

Ray's head is a cacophony of ideas. He needs to know how this Foster warlock can transfer himself into another body, and wants his secret. If he keeps the dog then he can hold it to ransom until Tommy returns to claim it. He'll chop the fucking thing up unless he tells him everything he knows. Now he's found out how much of a sissy Boinky is he needs to be careful how to play things.
He looks down at the dog just in time to see it yanked beneath the material of the tent by a litter grabber.

MATTHEW CASH

Chapter Fifty-Six

"What the hell?" Gloria asks as Norman thrusts a startled dachshund into her arms.
"You heard what they were saying. This dog is the answer to immortality," Norman grins at her excitedly and starts the mobility scooter up.
"Norman, stop," Ray yells as he runs out of the tent in time to see Norman take off across the grass.
Norman steers away from Ray and twists the throttle fully expecting the scooter to rocket at 1200cc speeds but it doesn't.
"Norman," Gloria whines, "he's catching up with us."
"I've fucked up, Glo, something's gone wrong, it won't accelerate." He twists the throttle again and swears profusely. Ray is cutting across the grass towards them, the scooter barely going faster than a walking pace.
"Just let him have the bloody dog, Norman, it's no good," Gloria says from behind him. "We've still got the other thing."
Georgina and Suki try their best to free themselves from Box, Boinky gives chase with Ray who lunges at the scooter. The dog whelps as Ray grabs a fistful of saggy skin and fur. Norman steers one-handed and thrusts his hand into the golf bag in front of him. Ray pulls Zoltan from Gloria's clutches. Norman hoists out a baseball bat and starts swinging it at the ringmaster.

MATTHEW CASH

Ray has the dog tucked beneath his arm like a rugby ball, he dodges Norman's attack and sees Boinky gaining on him. He really doesn't know what side Boinky is on now, and can't afford to let the clown give the dog back to the girls. The man who Tommy read last is ahead of him, leaning against his open car door, watching the commotion. Ray pushes him into the car, presses one of his sharp, silver-tipped fingers into the man's throat and orders him to drive.

The man protests at first but when Boinky rolls onto the bonnet and starts staring at them with red lit eyes he puts his foot down.

"What the bloody hell's going on?" Matt says steering from side to side to dislodge the disgruntled clown. Boinky clings on to the windscreen wipers for a few seconds but unsurprisingly they aren't strong enough to hold the weight of a twenty plus stone clown and one snaps off and Boinky bundles over the car and out of sight.

"Just do as you're told you won't get hurt," Ray leans back in the passenger seat cradling the dog.

"What are you doing? What are you going to do? Your fucking circus is nuts. One of your clowns assaulted me."

"I don't care."

Sensing no immediate danger from Ray Matt relaxed a bit. "Where am I going? Why do you have a dog with you?"

Ray grabs at his hair with one hand like he wants to yank it out. "I'm trying to think."

"'ere, I recognise that dog. He's the face of Humphries Pet se—"

"No, he isn't, he just looks the same."

"It fucking is. I'd recognise him anywhere. When we did the photo shoot he pissed everywhere."

FRANKIE SAYS DIE

"Okay, you've rumbled me," Ray turned to look out of the rear window. "Those people, they were trying to hurt him. Some deluded nonsense. They actually believe he has the spirit of a five hundred year old warlock inside him." Despite the fact that he was being held hostage Matt couldn't hold the laughter.

Ray grins. "I know right. I mean, could you pick a worse breed of dog to possess?" Ray stands the dog on its hind legs and jiggles the front paws with his hands. Zoltan just looks at Matt stupidly.

"What the hell can you do with this? If you were going to possess a dog would you choose a bloody dachshund?" Matt gives this some thought whilst driving at breakneck speed. "No, a chihuahua."

"Exactly," Ray says half-listening before acknowledging what the man said. "A chihuahua?"

"Yeah," Matt nods and gives him a quick grin. "I'd get one of those really hot supermodel types to carry me around in a little bag with her knickers in and watch her shower."

"And you say my circus is nuts?" Ray says disgustedly. "Find somewhere quiet we can hide out."

"Well, I was just going to the dog food factory. Your fortune teller reckoned I was going to invent a new flavour so I thought there was no time like the present."

"Okay, let's go save this pedigree, chum."

Chapter Fifty-Seven

"Where are they taking Zee?" Georgina cries tearing at her hair. She feels a giant hand rest on her shoulder and sees the unsettling, perpetually happy face of Boinky the clown. Suki's there to comfort her friend but it's Captain Flimbo who offers her reassurance.
"Don't worry, we'll sort this shit out."
Boinky waddles over to Box and something unheard is passed between them and Box hurries away. Boinky beckons the two girls to follow him as Captain Flimbo fills them in on the plan. "Boinky's told his kids to round up Tommy and catch up with us."
"We're going after them?" Suki asks, she sounds excited.
"Of course, Boinky has history with this fucker. He'll put this right, you mark my words. Time for you girl's to meet Persephone, Boinky's missus."
"Who the hell's Persephone?" Georgina asks.
The big clown hurries across the grass towards the car park where Boinky's rainbow campervan is parked. Boinky beams at them and points a finger. "That, is Persephone."
"Wait. Boinky's wife is a van?"
Boinky meets Suki's words with a knotted brow.
"Love is love," Captain Flimbo suggests.
"I don't care if he fucks the baby Jesus, let's get my dog!" Georgina storms ahead of them.
"I like her," Captain Flimbo says.
Boinky lets them in the van and before they've even sat down he's driving off in hot pursuit of Ray and Zoltan.

MATTHEW CASH

The circus performances are split between the two main tents now. Those with little kids would be in the biggest watching the jugglers, acrobats and other family-friendly acts, whilst everyone else was free to watch Rochelle's mini circus of horrors.

All four clowns receive Boinky's demand telepathically, a hive mind. Box scans the audience in the bigtop and can't see Tommy anywhere. Libby and Moopy are just about finished with their mother and baby act, the audience are in stitches as he does another ridiculously long projectile milk-vomit over Libby's gargantuan tits. Box is happy their show is nearly over, they can help him hunt for Tommy. Box leaves the family tent and heads over to the adult one where cheers and wolf whistles tell him that Rochelle and her girls are obviously performing, all tight, revealing PVC outfits and dangerous stuff. The tent is a lot smaller, Rochelle is wearing nothing but fishnets and stars, she's swinging to and from the audience, breathing flames over their heads, driving them insane. Mr Fumble is oiled up, his face painted like a skull and he's juggling machetes, eight of them, to the audience it looks amazing, they don't know about his invisible arms. Rochelle's dancers crack whips, swallow swords, and touch angle grinders against metallic cod-pieces and shower each other with sparks and sweat.
Box spots Tommy instantly, he's standing in the crowd gawping at the girls in bondage gear. There's no way Box can be subtle.

Frankie sees the big clown ploughing through the people like a human bulldozer and screams silently. The only exit

FRANKIE SAYS DIE

he can see lies beyond where the attack is coming from so he runs in the only direction he has left, the ring. His presence amidst the performance causes a stir, a few of the audience members recognise Tommy as The Boy Who Sees so think he's part of the act. Frankie grabs the handle of a sword that's sticking out of one of the sword-swallowers mouths. She flails her hands at him for a second, panic on her face, and then he yanks the long blade out in an arc of red. He spins and thrusts the sword through the chest of one of the other dancers, turns on one foot and disembowels another. The show stops and the screaming starts. Audience members trample over each other as Frankie slashes at them and the other dancers who advance on him to avenge their fallen sisters. Rochelle drops to the ground and Frankie uses this to his advantage. He presses the sword blade against her throat and grabs her from behind. She drops her flaming kevlar wick and bottle of fuel to the sand. He doesn't need to be able to talk, they know what he wants.

Box lands in the ring next to his brother who now stands like the goddess Kali at a Kiss concert, eight machetes ready to chop and dice. Box gestures for the dancers to get out. As the crowds leave the tent Libby and Moopy enter, the clown hive mind naturally calling them.

"You can't get anywhere, Tommy," Rochelle says squirming against the sword edge.

"Not Tommy," Box tells her. "Is bad man inside Tommy." Rochelle looks confused. Box tries harder to remember what he heard in the other tent. He points at the man behind her. "Is five hundred year witch, can swap bodies, live forever."

Rochelle slowly, and carefully, turned her face upward to look at Tommy. "Is this true?"

Frankie nods.

"They won't let you go, you know?" she says, "they aren't normal clowns." Then she adds, barely a whisper, "If you'll show me how to live forever I'll help you escape."

Frankie laughs silently at this, loves how people are so easy to double-cross one another. He's in a sticky situation and he knows it. He nods and drops the sword. Within seconds the skeletal face of Mr Fumble is leering at him and a hexagon of crossed machete blades surround his head.

Chapter Fifty-Eight

"Why has he brought him here?" Gloria says as Norman kills the scooter's lights and they watch Ray carry the little dog towards a dark building, the man he's with lets him in.
"I have no idea. What is this place?"
They were on an industrial estate, no life anywhere.
Gloria scanned the building and found a small sign saying Humphries Essentials. "Let's go and see what they're up to." Norman gets off the scooter, Gloria rushes around to help him.
"Have a look in the golf bag, Glo. There's some other stuff in there to protect us."

Ray follows Matt past conveyor belts and numerous machinery that all plays a part in the preparation and packaging of dog food. He leads them up a flight of stairs and into a small office which has a window overlooking the whole factory floor. The whole place is a lot smaller than Ray imagined. He eyes a switchboard on the wall.
"Can we turn the lights on? There's no point in hiding away. We know we're being followed."
Matt hits numerous switches and the whole factory is illuminated by floodlights high above the factory floor. Ray sees Norman and his wife scurry behind some boxes. "We are not alone, Mr Humphries."
"Eh?" Matt says scanning the factory floor.
"A troublesome OAP and his wife."

MATTHEW CASH

"What do they want? Are they part of this witchy bollocks?"

"You are so eloquent. Yes, yes they are. There are a few of these deluded individuals unfortunately, who want to hurt this poor little doggy." Ray pats Zoltan on the head and he just slops his jaws lazily in response.

"What do they want to do with him, worship him or something?"

"It's a lot worse than that I'm afraid." Ray positions Zoltan on his lap so Matt can see him better. "They want to cut out his liver whilst he's still awake and make someone else eat it to transfer the soul of the warlock into that person."

"The dirty, dirty, bastards," Matt growled. If there was one thing he couldn't abide it was animal cruelty. "Fucking pigs. If they lay their hands on him I'll throw them in the fucking meat grinder."

Ray clapped a hand on his shoulder. "Glad to have you on my side," he pauses, deep in thought. "Tell me about this meat grinder."

"I can't believe that guy who Ray went with was the dog food guy," Georgina whispers to Suki in the back of Persephone.

"Yeah, it's a remarkable coincidence, isn't it?" Suki says picking at a crusty lump on the seat covering. The interior of the van is decked out in thick, pink fur, a lot of it is matted together in suspicious clumps. She can't help but think about the vehicle being the clown's wife. She wipes her hands rapidly on her trousers. "Do you think he's involved in all this or it's just some convenient way to bring this whole farcical adventure to an end?"

"Yeah sure," Georgina scoffs, "if this was just a ridiculous story being written by some dickhead who's twice our age

FRANKIE SAYS DIE

with a horror fixation who thinks he's fucking funny and doesn't have the imagination to connect his scenes in any better way. But it's not, it's the fucking real world, baby, and my dog has a five hundred year old warlock's liver inside him and is the key to his resurrection."
"He's definitely shat it out by now."
"You what?"
"The liver."
"Yeah, well I don't suppose that matters much now he has his hold over Zee."
"Why do you think Ray's dognapped him?"
"Isn't it obvious? He's going to hold my dog to ransom so this dude, who's currently riding Tommy like a bucking bronco, shows up. Probably wants to know how it's done. Wouldn't you?"
Suki thinks on this and can't deny that she's more than a little bit intrigued to witness the whole process but whether she would actually want to participate in the ritual herself is another matter.
"I don't even know if I'm crazy enough to self-mutilate myself for the chance of swapping my decrepit old body for a new one."
"Yeah, but what if you knew it worked? What if you meticulously chose a new body? Spent ages and ages searching for the perfect host to take over?" Georgina waves her hands smugly over herself like she is flaunting the star prize on a quiz show.
"Yeah, I really don't know why he picked you."
Georgina doesn't really know why the warlock formally known as The Smiler chose her, it's not like her body has any attributes other than youthfulness and a slight

knowledge of kickboxing that for all she knew might not actually transfer with the soul-swap.

"We're there," Captain Flimbo shouts from Boinky's gut breaking Georgina from her reverie. She peers out of the window and sees they're in a darkened industrial estate. For a moment she thinks the clown must be wrong but she spots the dog food guy's car parked next to a mobility scooter. Suki and Georgina get out of Persephone and wait for Boinky to finish whatever he's doing behind the steering wheel.

The windows begin to fog up and they hear Captain Flimbo cackle, "You dirty bastard, that went in my eye."

"I don't want to know," Georgina turns abruptly and faces the building. There's a door open so she walks towards it. Suki follows.

"Wait," Captain Flimbo calls, and Boinky comes hurtling out of the VW and stops in front of them. "It might be dangerous." From seemingly out of nowhere Boinky magics up a long, wide, butcher's knife, it gleams in the street lamps and the girls can see funny little runes etched into its blade. Boinky holds it to his tattooed lips and either kisses it or whispers something and the knife sprouts dragonfly wings and begins to buzz around him excitedly.

"Dude has a flying knife," Suki states the obvious.

"Nothing else will ever surprise me." Georgina steps aside as Boinky sends the knife through the doorway like some bizarre sniffer dog. He follows and leads them into the building.

It's a factory. Boxes of pet food are stacked in crates everywhere. All the lights are on and there's the steady hum of machinery. Georgina sees the dog food man looking out of a little window above the factory floor, sees

FRANKIE SAYS DIE

him lean over something and then his voice fills the building.
"Don't come any closer."
There are speakers dotted around all over the place, cameras too most likely.
"Where's my dog?" Georgina yells.
Boinky's knife rockets off into the dark recesses.
"Boinky, reel Jonathan back in or the dog gets it." Ray. His voice comes from somewhere on the other side of the factory.
Captain Flimbo whistles and there's a quick rush of air and the knife is back whizzing around his shoulders.
"Ray," Georgina yells again, "what have you done with my dog?"
"He's fine. He's safe," Ray calls. "We can't let Tommy get near him."
Georgina tries to locate Ray by the sound of his voice. She ducks under machinery and conveyor belts.

Zoltan is bound in rope, hanging above a huge and nasty looking piece of machinery. She runs towards him but just as she's about to touch his paw he is pulled up high in the air. Ray appears on a platform, the controls of whatever this contraption is in his hand. "One more step and he's churned into dog food."
"What the fuck, you sick bastard," Georgina cries up at him, Zoltan yelps down at her.
"I'm trying to save your dog, believe it or not."
"You've got him hanging over a mincer!" Suki screams, her liking for the ringmaster was rapidly vanishing.
"To lure Frankie."

Georgina laughs. "Then what?"

Ray saddens and stares into the whirring metal teeth. "There's no other way."

"No, you are not killing my dog."

"If he goes into the mincer with Frankie inside him it will end it."

"What if Frankie whips into Tommy?"

Ray shakes his head, "He can't stay in Tommy permanently, eventually he will be rejected and have nowhere to go. He has to occupy the host that partook in the ritual."

Georgina exchanges glances with Boinky and Suki. Suki steps forward and raises her hand. "Doesn't someone need to speak the ritual for it to work?"

Ray nods. "Yes, and nobody knows the words apart from Frankie and possibly Tommy."

"So, if we killed Tommy—"

"Woh, Suke, no one is killing anyone." A smile spreads across Georgina's face. "If Tommy doesn't say the words for him he'll have to stay inside Zee. We'll have to find him another vessel or something."

"Like a Chucky doll?"

Georgina grimaces, "But that's still going to involve cutting my dog's liver out."

"What a fucking palaver," Captain Flimbo sighs for want of something to say.

"Oh, fuck this for a game of soldiers," someone growls and Georgina feels herself grabbed from behind and something sharp pressed against her throat.

"I was wondering when you were going to show yourself," Ray grins down at Norman.

Chapter Fifty-Nine

Zoltan doesn't know what the flying fuck is going on. There's loads of strange people picking him up without even letting him sniff them first and he misses the floaty feeling when he felt just like he did as a puppy and he could run around the silly dog that looked just like him. He was back to feeling old and tired and hurty again. Everything hurt, all of his bones. When the funny-smelling man wrapped rope around his middle and hung him in the air it sort of felt nice, like early morning back stretches. He could smell his mistress nearby even though his eyes had gone back to being all cloudy. He hoped she would come and get him soon so they could cuddle under blankets.

Tommy hovers above the cab of the Greenfield circus truck, knows Frankie is in his body and there's nothing he can do to stop him until he pops back into the dog. The lorry pulls up outside an industrial unit and Rochelle leaps from the cab followed by the four clowns, she holds a sword out towards their prisoner. Box shoves him towards the factory

There's some sort of ruckus, shouting, swearing. It pulls Rochelle's attention away from the group she has now taken charge of. High up above some wicked looking piece of machinery Ray stands on a platform with the little dog wrapped up like a fly in a web. Below, the unmistakable bulk of Boinky virtually eclipses the two girls he stands behind. An older couple gathers with them, a man has his arm wrapped around the white haired girl, a machete pressed against the pale curve of her neck.

Fuck. Frankie wants to scream it from the top of Tommy's lungs. It's over. He can feel his hold over Tommy weakening, knows he needs to swap back into the dog, but what then?

"Ah," Ray says beckoning to Rochelle and the clowns. "The gang's all here at last."
Boinky turns to look at them and for a moment his eyes flicker red.
Ray waggles the hanging controls of the mincer in Frankie's direction. "I think it's high time we started discussing some kind of solution to all this don't you?"
"Make him say the words or I'll cut this girl's head off," Norman shouts.
"You tell him, Norman," Gloria coerced from his side, keeping one eye on the other girl, a long, three-pronged barbecue fork poking in her ribs.
"Now, now, Norman, no need for that yet." Ray addressed his wife, "Could you bring Tommy up here please so we can get everyone back to their rightful bodies?"
Rochelle thrusts her sword towards a set of stairs leading up to the platform and follows Box as he frogmarches Tommy up to Ray.

He can't help it. Being this close to the dog makes him automatically zap back into the bound canine. He gives Tommy a second to get adjusted to being back in his own body again before telepathically carolling him. *Tommy, you've got to help me.*

FRANKIE SAYS DIE

"Why the fuck should I help you?" Tommy splutters, his body feels ancient after the bliss of being in spirit form.
"Are you talking to...?" Ray points at the dachshund who has locked eyes with him.
Tommy points at the dog. "I'm talking to him. He wants me to help him."
Ray nods. "Maybe there's a way we can help each other."
"No," Tommy says, "there's no way out of this without killing Georgina's dog and Frankie knows it. We all know it."
"You bastard," Georgina has tears in her eyes, she knows what Tommy says is true.
Norman roars with the frustration of it all. "Say the words or I'll fucking kill her."
"I truly underestimated you, Norman," Ray says and pulls a long knife from his belt. He slashes at the rope holding the dog and places it, still bound, on the platform. "Bring her up here."
"Keep hold of her," Norman says to Gloria who tightens her grip on Suki as he hobbles up the stairs on his ruined legs.
It takes him forever.
"Looks like there's no choice other than to perform the rite, Tommy," Ray sounds sympathetic.
Tommy, listen to me, it's the only way. Frankie says from the dachshund. *Just say the words. Once I'm in the girl we'll kill everyone and get out of here.*
But it's not fair, Tommy communicates without making a sound.
I tell you what, we'll share the body, come to some arrangement. You have my word.

MATTHEW CASH

Tommy can't believe what he's hearing but as the old man forces Georgina to the platform he realises there aren't a lot of choices left.

"Okay," Tommy says to everyone.

"No, Tommy," Georgina cries.

"I'm sorry."

As soon as Tommy begins to say the words Frankie knows he's fucked up royally. There was a chance that they wouldn't work at all because the person who was making the transference wasn't saying the words themselves but it's now that he's found out that the words work independently. It doesn't matter who says them just as long as they are said. All this time, one of his victims, if they had been in the knowhow, could have force-fed him a part of their liver and swapped into him.

Norman feels a tingling from within him as Tommy speaks the foreign words.

Ray cackles. "I knew it. I knew it."

Everyone there feels the same sensation, the magic has taken root in their livers.

Ray beams down at Rochelle and the clowns. "Kill them all."

"But the chant?"

Ray pulls his mobile phone from his pocket, presses it a few times and Tommy's voice comes from the speaker.

"I've got everything we need. It's the words that are magic not the warlock. Kill them."

Frankie zips back into Tommy before he has a chance to react and kicks Rochelle squarely in the face sending her back down the stairs into Box. Ray swipes at him with his knife but he ducks and plants a fist right in his solar plexus.

FRANKIE SAYS DIE

Suki pulls away from Gloria and they just stare at each other in awkward confusion.
"I don't want to fight you," Suki whines.
Gloria seems to see the barbecue fork for the first time.
"This is a right mess isn't it?"
Mr Fumble springs to the floor in front of them and resumes his Kali impression he did at the circus. He's a whirlwind of blades. With his eight arms he'll slice them and dice them in seconds.

Frankie grabs hold of the mincer controls, gets the things started and pushes Ray towards the edge of the platform. Ray's phone keeps playing Frankie's mantra over and over again.

Norman spots Ray's fallen knife, knocks Georgina to the floor and rips open his shirt whilst holding the machete against her throat. He picks the knife up and screams out in pain as he drags the blade across his stomach.

Boinky stands back and watches everything go up shit creek. His children are all bloodthirsty morons, all four of them are ready to tear Suki and Gloria apart, the older woman somehow keeping them at bay with a puny fork, Frankie is using Tommy to pummel the living shit out of Ray and drag him closer and closer to the edge of the platform with the obvious intention of chucking him in the mincer, there's a random bloke gawping at the lot of them through a tiny office window and to be quite honest Boinky has had enough. He can feel it starting in his own belly, not a reaction to Frankie's magic, the only spell that old warlock used on him was the one that beckoned him here to this universe. No, he can feel his forevermouth waking like a sleepy dragon.

"Ball's in your court, Boinko m'lad," Captain Flimbo says sadly. Boinky doesn't quite understand this modern lingo the Captain has picked up on but as they're connected he gets his meaning.

Boinky can't undo Frankie's magic, for some reason that's against whatever rules are in play here and he can't hurt the one who brought him here. He has been here a long time, knows who is innocent and who isn't. The girls, Tommy, the cute little doggy, the lady who has an invisible black spider inside her that these humans call cancer. He can save them all, if he wants to, apart from the dog who is bound to Frankie.

He solemnly slumps onto his great doughy buttocks and lets the forevermouth open.

Georgina scrabbles away from Norman as he drops the knife to thrust his hand inside himself. He looks at her and grins through a mouthful of blood. "It doesn't hurt." He yanks out pieces of himself and realises he has no fucking idea where his liver is let alone what it looks like. He falls to his knees and just starts pulling everything out, she can't believe what she is seeing. He's literally tearing himself apart to live longer. He holds a bloody lump out towards her and starts sobbing with insanity. "Is this my liver?" Georgina breaks away from him and crouches over Zoltan and begins to untie his binds. An unearthly roar drowns out the noise of the machinery and the mantra recording and she finds its source on the factory floor.

There's a black and red swirling vortex where Boinky's head should be and it seems to be sucking everything

FRANKIE SAYS DIE

toward it. It reminds her of a mobile phone game where you have to be this giant mouth and eat everything. Anything that isn't nailed down gets sucked into that wormhole and Georgina begins to feel the tug on the gravity around her. She sees one of the clowns, the baby one, fly into the hole. For a second the woman one stares mournfully after it before she too is absorbed. The clown with the invisible arms is next, he somersaults over Suki and Gloria who don't seem to be affected by the pull. "No!" Ray screams.

Georgina turns and sees Frankie finally push the ringmaster into the dog food mincer but he doesn't hit the blades, he flies over it, caught in the trajectory of the portal. Ray clamps hold of the stair rail, the only thing in the factory beside the mincer that seems to be staying put and shouts behind him, "Not me, Boinky." He knows what the clown is doing, cleaning up, it's all he ever does. He sees Rochelle lose her grip on Box's ankle and shriek off into oblivion. "Shit, Boinky, that hurt."

Box is clinging to some heavy piece of machinery, determined not to be taken by his father. Rivets and screws fly past his head as the machine is pulled apart but still the strong clown hangs on. Then there's a sickening rip and the skin from his exposed back half is slurped from his bones by some unseen tongue, he too is taken.

Norman's slumped body is dragged across the platform and it's headed straight for Ray. The heavy old man collides with him, his gaping stomach wound swallowing his head and knocking him from the stair rail. Ray feels himself rocket backwards and experiences the ice-cold sensation of deep space before he explodes.

MATTHEW CASH

Frankie claws his way across the platform, the mobile phone in his hand. Ray has done him a favour with the recording. Below Boinky has returned back to his usual state. As Frankie suspected, he can't harm the one who conjured him.

Georgina has unfastened Zoltan and she can tell it's really him due to the sadness in his eyes. He licks at her face and she hugs him to her chest. A hand clamps around her ankle. Frankie pulls her towards him. She lets go of Zoltan and tells him to run, run, run. Frankie crawls on top of her and tries to reach out for the dog. She drives her knee into his balls and he doesn't even notice it. She wraps her arms around him to prevent him using Tommy's body to get to Zoltan. "Run!" she screams at her stupid dog who still hasn't run off. He's just standing there staring at the whirring blades beneath him.

Determined Frankie pushes Tommy's body to its limits, he doesn't care if he destroys it in the process. The dog is mere inches away now, all he has to do is cut out the liver and give it to the girl but then the dog does something ridiculously stupid that only the most dickheadest of dogs would do.

Zoltan really wants the shiny, whirry things, they look really tasty and they smell tasty, like Humphries dog food, his favourite. Even though his old body is tired and hurty he gives his best jump.

It was instinctive, Frankie saw the vessel that contained the answer to his near-immortality, and jumped into it

FRANKIE SAYS DIE

thinking he could somehow make the dog spin in midair and avoid the churning nightmare beneath him. Frankie realises his error immediately and attempts to swap back but as he's racing out of the dog, leaving it to the grinder, he sees Georgina roll the unsuspecting Tommy off herself and down he comes too.

Georgina sits above the blades and watches her tears fall into the mixture. "I love you, Zoltan," she whispers. She hears footsteps behind her and someone switches the mincer off. Suki puts her arms around her. Georgina leans into her friend and sees Boinky standing beside a tearful, shaking Gloria.

Frankie hates being a ghost, he knows it's only temporary, can feel the pull of the other side already and he really doesn't want to know where he's going. He flutters towards the girls and Gloria but there's no way inside any of them. A quick scout around the factory shows him there's nothing at all to help him out, no weak-willed rodent he can possess whilst he thinks about how to get himself out of this fix, nothing. He clocks the clown looking at him and knows there's no chance that fucker will help him. He can feel himself dissipating. It's all over. But then he catches the alien whiff of something, it's coming from the old woman, her cancer. Frankie quickly dips a toe into the spreading mass and finds himself anchored. He would never have guessed that this would work. With a ghostly cackle at Boinky, he dives headfirst into Gloria's gut.

Gloria suddenly bursts into action, jabs Boinky in the belly with the barbecue fork and races down the stairs.
"What the fuck?" Suki says.
Boinky pulls the fork from his stomach and rolls his eyes.
"Fuck's sake," Captain Flimbo groans. "You don't want to fucking know."

FRANKIE SAYS DIE

Epilogue

It was handy, what with there being no evidence as such, Matt Humphries thought as he checked the figures for the new flavour of dog food. Just as the fortune-teller predicted, it was a blinding seller, especially with him being part of the ingredients. It was a shame about the little dog though. Matt didn't really understand what the hell went on at the factory and the three women and the clown had vanished something sharpish afterwards. All that mumbo-jumbo about soul-swapping and liver-eating. Probably a bunch of fucking hippies.

"There's someone selling puppies for £1000," Suki says reading from an article on her phone. "Dachshunds."
"Suke," Georgina sighs and leans against the manga shop counter, "I can't. Zee was everything to me. I can't go through that again."
Suki was about to close the search engine window when one of the dachshund results caught her eye. It was a news article, recent, about a spate of the adorable little weiner dogs going missing from their homes. At first people thought they had been stolen but there were actual eyewitnesses from owners who saw their once-loyal dogs ignore them and run away. This was happening in random places over the county and not just dachshunds either. The only thing they had in common was they had all recently swapped to a new flavour of Humphries' dog food. Their

owners were trying to say there was some additive in the limited edition batch that had sent their dogs crazy.

Suki reaches out, grabs Georgina and thrusts her phone towards her.

"Look," Georgina starts, expecting to see yet another nest of adorable dachshund puppies her friend was trying to get her to fall for but then both of them get distracted by the noise.

Car horns honking and a cacophony of barking.

"What the fuck?" Georgina rushes from the counter and they both run through the door.

There are dogs everywhere, dozens, of all shapes, sizes and breeds. When they see her they run around in circles of happiness.

"What's going on, Suke?"

Suki shows her the article.

Georgina gapes at the pack of dogs, crouches and smiles. "Zee?"

They all bark with one voice as Zoltan rushes to meet his owner.

FRANKIE SAYS DIE

Author Biography

Matthew Cash, or Matty-Bob Cash as he is known to most, was born and raised in Suffolk, which is the setting for his debut novel Pinprick. He is compiler and editor of Death by Chocolate, a chocoholic horror Anthology and the 12Days: STOCKING FILLERS Anthology. In 2016 he launched his own publishing house Burdizzo Books and took shit-hot editor and author Em Dehaney on board to keep him in shape and together they brought into existence SPARKS: an electrical horror anthology, The Reverend Burdizzo's Hymn Book, Under the Weather* Visions from the Void ** and The Burdizzo Mix Tape Vol. 1.
He has numerous solo releases on Kindle and several collections in paperback.
Originally with Burdizzo Books, the intention was to compile charity anthologies a few times a year but his creation has grown into something so much more powerful *insert mad laughter here*. He is currently working on numerous projects; The Day Before You Came is his sixth novel
. *With Back Road Books
** With Jonathan Butcher
He has always written stories since he first learnt to write and most, although not all, tend to slip into the many-layered murky depths of the Horror genre.
His influences ranged from when he first started reading to Present day are, to name but a small select few; Roald Dahl, James Herbert, Clive Barker, Stephen King, Stephen Laws, and more recently he enjoys Adam Nevill, F.R Tallis, Michael Bray, Gary Fry, William Meikle and Iain Rob

MATTHEW CASH

Wright (who featured Matty-Bob in his famous A-Z of Horror title M is For Matty-Bob, plus Matthew wrote his own version of events which was included as a bonus). He is a father-of-two, a husband-of-one, and a zookeeper of numerous fur babies.

You can find him here:
www.facebook.com/pinprickbymatthewcash
https://www.amazon.co.uk/-/e/B010MQTWKK
www.burdizzobooks.com

FRANKIE SAYS DIE

Other Releases by Matthew Cash

Novels

Virgin and the Hunter
Pinprick
Fur
Your Frightful Spirit Stayed
The Glut
The Day Before You Came

Novellas

Ankle Biters
KrackerJack
Illness
Hell, and Sebastian
Waiting For Godfrey
Deadbeard
The Cat Came Back
KrackerJack 2
Werwolf
Frosty
Keida-in-the-Flames
Tesco agogo

Short Stories

Why Can't I Be You?
Slugs and Snails and Puppydog Tails
Oldtimers

MATTHEW CASH
Hunt The C*nt
Clinton Reed's FAT

Anthologies Compiled and Edited by Matthew Cash & Em Dehaney

Death by Chocolate
12 Days: STOCKING FILLERS
12 Days: 2016 Anthology
12 Days: 2017
The Reverend Burdizzo's Hymn Book
Sparks
Welcome To A Town Called Hell
VISIONS FROM THE VOID (with Jonathan Butcher)
Under the Weather (with Back Road Books)
Burdizzo Mix Tape Vol.1
Beneath The Leaves

Anthologies Featuring Matthew Cash

Rejected For Content 3: Vicious Vengeance
JEApers Creepers
Full Moon Slaughter
Full Moon Slaughter 2
Freaks
No Place Like Home: Twisted Tales from the Yellow Brick Road
Down The Rabbit Hole: Tales of Insanity

Collections

Stromboli And Other Sporadic Eruptions

FRANKIE SAYS DIE

Printed in Great Britain
by Amazon